Sherlock Holmes and the Jade Statuette

with other strange stories

By

Jim Watson

Dedicated to my lifelong friend
Richard Kurcewicz
 and our early interest in all things musical,
mathematical and literary

Also available on Amazon Kindle

The Monkey in the Machine
The Monkey, the Machine and the Sentinel
The Stalybridge Tragedy and my later
Life.
Karma Comedy: Kafka on the Blue Train
Quigley goes North
Quigley in Trouble
Eastman's Retreat
Eastman in the Desert
The Killerbowl: New York Nightmare 2090
The True History of the Dearborn Chainsaw Murders
The Night Tinkerbell died
The Dragon of Wu Pi

for more details of these works please see back of book page 198

4

Contents

5

Sherlock Holmes and the Jade Statuette

(from the memoirs of Dr John H Watson, being previously unpublished)

It being Easter Sunday, I had called upon my friend
Sherlock Holmes with the intention of passing the
afternoon in his company. Like many others I always
found Sundays and Bank Holidays to be tedious affairs, so
to break the Sabbatical monotony a change was always
welcome. The weather was dull and overcast and already
a light rain was falling as I strode down Baker Street to
the familiar door of Mrs Hudson's lodgings for gentlemen
at 221B.

An unfamiliar scullery maid answered my knock and,
when I asked if my old colleague was at home, showed
me up the stairs to Holmes's chambers on the first floor,
no doubt thinking me a stranger. I did not trouble myself
to knock but walked right in to his rooms only to find him
reclining on the chaise longue that stood near the window.

Holmes was dressed in a Tartan pattern woollen dressing gown, a fact I put down to the unseasonable chill in the air. A discarded breakfast tray lay upon the floor within easy reach of where he was sitting. The tray spoke of Mrs Hudson's absence from the establishment for the hour was advancing towards two in the afternoon. That it was a breakfast tray was apparent from the presence of a jar of Frank Cooper's excellent marmalade. The great man had something in his hand that he was studying by means of a large magnifying glass.

'Ah Holmes!' said I by way of an informal greeting. 'You are busy, perhaps I am interrupting you?'

With that easy charm which I always found so captivating his face abandoned its former studious mien and lit up in a genuine smile. 'Watson, Watson, how nice to see you. Come in, sit down.' As he said this he rose to his feet putting down the object he had been studying. With his usual courtesy and solicitousness he then prevailed upon me to take a seat near the fire which, by means of skilful use of the poker, he soon had merrily blazing. He then made a fresh pot of tea taking water from the kettle that always sang in its position at the side of the fire. We passed the usual pleasantries back and forth as we waited for the tea to brew and I warmed my hands at the fire. Once he had poured my tea he returned to the study of the object he left lying on the chaise longue.

'Mary is away. Her sister, a veritable goddess of fertility has produced yet another child.' I told of my wife's absence in my temporary status as a bachelor gay.

'Let me see if I can remember,' he mused. 'Your wife Mary's sister is called Prudence, which is something she apparently lacks in certain quarters. I assume the new child is yet another girl making a total of five?'

'Holmes, you astound me. You have the memory of an elephant by George! How some ever, things being a trifle dull at home I thought to essay here in search of amusement my dear fellow.'

This sally only drew a monosyllabic 'Hmmh' from the detective so I went off on another tangent. 'I venture to presume that Mrs Hudson is away from home?'

Holmes continued to scrutinise the object which I now saw to be a statuette made of a variety of some green mineral or other. It depicted some obscure, possibly Chinese, female deity and was about nine inches high.

While continuing to focus his attention upon the statue Holmes spoke again. 'From which observations did you base your deduction concerning the whereabouts of the splendid proprietress of these premises? I am always willing to learn something new, perhaps you could enlighten me?'

9

Then without pausing to allow me to reply he went on. 'No doubt before joining me you took the opportunity to examine her bedroom, and found clothes and a suitcase to be missing? Or perhaps your cousin Gertrude bumped into Mrs Hudson on the promenade at Eastbourne and immediately sent you a telegram to the effect?'

Challenged to explain my observations I replied as follows, 'No Holmes. It was a mere supposition based on two casual observations. Mrs Hudson generally answers the door herself unless otherwise occupied, and when I came in, I could not help but notice the presence of the breakfast tray on the floor. Mrs Hudson would never place such a tray upon the floor and there was also the fact that the time has now advanced to five after two. A trifle late for breakfast? Hey!'

Holmes ceased looking at the effigy and raised his eyebrows looking directly at me. 'Really? Quite! Yes! Very impressive, but - -'

At that moment came a knock on the door.

'Come!' called Holmes, and in the next couple of seconds we were treated to the imperious presence of Mrs Hudson herself who glided into the room. She smiled to acknowledge my presence then stopped to inquire after my health and that of Mary my wife. She then walked over to the chaise longue that Holmes had now re-occupied.

'You'll be finished with your lunch now, Mr Holmes I take it?'

'Breakfast, surely Mrs Hudson,' with a good humoured twinkle in his eye, 'one does not usually lunch upon boiled eggs, toast and marmalade?'

Fixing Holmes with a censorious eye the stoical lady replied, 'Neither did other gentlemen I have served, take their breakfasts at one o clock off the floor. Mr Holmes.' Having delivered this combination of a reproof and a riposte she picked up the tray and swept out of the room.

Holmes, who always had a puckish sense of humour, derived much enjoyment from the little exchange with his redoubtable landlady.

'As a matter of interest, old chap, why did you take your breakfast so late. And in such a Bohemian manner?' I inquired.

'Simplicity itself. I dined with Sir Hector Vernon last night in the Albany. He has a wonderful collection of Indian artefacts including some Thugee scarves – fascinating if gruesome. He also has some wonderful Chateau Lafitte and his crusted Port is beyond reproach.'

'You were late home?'

'Almost too late to be late, more like excessively early – so I overslept.'

'That is an ample explanation for the late breakfast but not your preference for eating from a tray on the floor?'

'Convenience and time saving, the two great gods of modern times, Watson! The sofa you will observe is well lit for it adjoins the window, whereas the dining table rests in a dark corner of the room.'

'Ah the light has dawned my dear chap. By adopting your position upon the chaise longue you could combine mastication of your food and examination of the Objet d'art in equal measures.'

'Succinctly put Watson.'

Arising from my position near the fire I walked over to Holmes to take a closer look at the piece of finely wrought green stone which he still grasped. He gravely handed it over so I could look at it more closely. 'This is an effigy of Guan Yin, if I am not mistaken. Goddess of Mercy and Compassion I believe? But I suppose,' I remarked, not without a trace of pride in my own erudition, 'that this beautiful piece of Jade has a tale of vice, depravity and violence attached to it?'

'It is not impossible,' began Holmes, 'that in a city such as this which teems with four million of us, "jostling each others elbows" so to speak, sprinkled as we are with people of all races and nations of the Empire, not to say

other parts of the world, that violence and vice should rub
shoulders with gentility and virtue.'

'So the clue to this outburst of violence is contained in
this statuette I suppose?' I said as I handed it back to the
great man.

'A man was killed and found holding this pathetic object.'
Saying this Holmes threw the magnifying glass to one
corner of the room and the statue to another. He gave an
expression to his disgust when I narrowly caught the
effigy before it hit the carpet.

'Holmes, really! Have a care. This thing may well be
quite valuable and I am sure it does not belong to you.'

'Valuable? A piece of manufactured trumpery is all it is.
A collector would turn up his nose at it. If you saw it on a
stall at Petticoat Lane you would not venture more than
half a sovereign.'

'I find it quite attractive.'

'Well keep it Watson, it won't be missed at the scene of
the crime.' Pleased I placed it on the mantel piece above
the fire, hoping I would notice it later and remember to
take it home with me. Holmes continued, striding about
the room as he spoke.
'A certain Mr. Zhang, a prosperous importer of Oriental
bric a brac, was found early yesterday morning with a
crushed skull. In his hand was the object that now adorns

the mantelpiece. Examination by the constabulary soon established that the place had been broken into, no doubt with felonious intent. But the strange aspect of the case is that the body of Mr Zhang was found in a locked room, which was also barred with two sliding bolts from the inside.'

'So whoever broke in would have been unable to get to Mr Zhang because the room he was in was locked off from the rest of the premises? But the gentleman in question still turned up dead?'

'Extremely.' Holmes confirmed. 'In fact the police doctor established that by the time the body was discovered Mr Zhang had been dead for at least eight hours. However our remarkable constabulary immediately solved the enigma by arresting his eldest son.'

'Well! I suppose somebody must have done it, and the poor chap did have the virtue of proximity. Why may I ask have your services been requested in such an open and shut case?'

'I venture to suggest, my friend, that given the circumstances, this is more of a shut case than an open one.' I thought this to be an excellent jest and laughed heartily.

Holmes strode to the window and looked out. 'I do believe that the weather is clearing up. Shall we go out for a stroll? Mrs Hudson has come into the possession of a large leg of Venison so the repast later on should be worth staying on for. I shall ask her to put up a plate for you my dear chap. I shall just stroll into the bedroom and change into some more suitable apparel. But before he could do this there came a knock on his door. The little malnourished looking tweenie, who had shown me in earlier, came in with another young lady in her wake.

'Beggin' your pardon sir. But this lady would like to speak to you. I told her that you don't work for nuffink but she will insist and it being Easter Sunday too!' said the maid in somewhat censorious tones.

Holmes and I exchanged frustrated glances, but there was nothing for it but to comply with the demands of his profession so I took another seat by the fire and began to pour myself another cup of tea.

'May I have the pleasure of knowing your name Maam?'

'My name is Beryl Lawson,' said the sombrely dressed young woman who wore a fustian grey short cloak over a black cotton dress that had seen better days. She wore 'sensible' boots and on her head was a short black bonnet of the sort favoured by the Salvationists. My eyes beheld a pretty young woman with a good figure but whose pale features bore the marks of recent privation.

'Do take a seat and advise how I can help' Holmes brought up one of the chairs that had been positioned close to the fire place. He then apologised for his dishabille and excused himself before going through into his bedroom to change.

'I'm Watson, by the way,' said I. The girl gave a nervous cough, glanced in my direction and then looked away. 'Friend and helper you know! Why me and Holmes go back quite a few years now, but not so much these days. I am a physician, a practice in Malden now being my home.' After these and a few other common places I managed to bring a smile to the rather handsome features of this young lady. It was obvious from her posture that she was in rather a 'state of nerves' as the modern phrase has it.

Holmes returned suitably attired for business and in a few short questions drew most of the essential information out from Miss Lawson.

'I have a post as a governess to a family in Whalley Range, Manchester. Jewish people, but very respectable in the cloth trade. They have been very kind in allowing me this leave of absence, but they cannot keep my position open indefinitely.'

'I told them a lie, Mr Holmes, making up a fictional Aunt Agatha who lived in London, sick and alone. I came here and found the cheapest lodgings available. I have been wandering around the docks for the last four weeks looking for him. But now -'

'You have run out of money and time? But I assume that you have the wherewithal to pay my fees?'

'I was told that your usual charge is three guineas?'

In his best manner, that would have done credit to a medical man, he prised more of the story out of her. 'It is no good,' she said. 'I will not see him again, we were not fated for each other.'

'Perhaps if you were to begin at the beginning. It is generally best, even if you have to repeat a few things,' he then turned to me winking quickly. 'Ah Watson would you mind going downstairs and asking Mrs Hudson what is delaying our lunch. Do inform her that we are both famished, and ask her to work her usual miracles.'

'Certainly, Holmes' I said and sprang to the door to do his bidding. This was very compassionate of him because it was obvious that young Miss Lawson was badly in need of some sustenance.

I had only returned from my mission for ten minutes when the little tweenie arrived at the door with a very decent spread of food consisting of slices of cheese and ham, buttered bread, a pot of jam, and no less than half a dozen scones. She took our tea pot and retired downstairs only to return with a larger one, three tea cups, milk and sugar and tea plates.

Holmes displayed all the symptoms of shock and surprise before exclaiming,'Really Watson you'd have thought the Mrs Hudson would have remembered that I have to abstain from Ham and Cheese on Easter Sunday.'

'Mr Holmes is very religious,' I explained to the young lady.

'Send them back then,' said Miss Lawson, 'I am sure some other gentleman in the house would appreciate them.'

'Oh dear no! We can't afford to offend Mrs Hudson. She is a tigress when roused. You and the doctor here will have to eat them for it would never do for her to discover that the food had not been eaten.'

This ruse worked admirably for once the young lady conquered her initial shyness she proceeded to demolish the contents of the tray like a trencherman. It was obvious that she had not eaten anything substantial in days. I had to, of course, pretend to eat the odd thing, but I made sure that she consumed most of the food. Holmes having observed the demeanour and deportment of the young client extemporised as follows.

'So to summarise, my dear, you have been keeping company with a young man of a nautical bent who has made certain declarations to you. You had not seen him for a few days and became anxious. With your sailor fiancée, having been missing from his lodgings in

Ardwick for two weeks, you inquired at the Mission and were told that he had departed for Liverpool. When you arrived in Liverpool you went straight to the docks and discovered that the ship he was supposed to board had left port, disappointed you returned to Manchester.

You yourself are not a Mancunian but originate from Oldham, where your family still remain. Your father is a foreman in a nearby Cotton Spinning factory, but your mother teaches at a Board School. You were a bright and diligent pupil and won a scholarship to the Mather College of Education in Manchester, where you obtained a teaching certificate which enabled you to take up your current post as a governess.

The young lady was so awe struck by this recital that she nearly, but not quite, ceased to eat from the bounteous tray.

' - and incidentally, your employer's mother – or father has recently passed away, because you are dressed in secondary mourning. You have been staying in cheap lodgings in Camden for two weeks, where you have been starving yourself and finally after having paid your landlady off you have only five guineas to your person and a return ticket to Manchester from Euston.'

'I do declare that you are wonder Mr Holmes,' said Miss Lawson, 'but how did you manage to reach so many accurate conclusions based on the barest details.'

'I will not bore you with my methods, these things are plain to see if one has the eyes to see them, but the fact is Miss Lawson, that you have been cruelly deceived.'

'Mr Holmes -No!' Her pale features assumed an even more ashen cast as she reacted to this terrible news.

The great detective now with his best bedside manner began to minister to the hurt feelings of the young lady who had entrusted £150 of her savings to a man calling himself Godfrey Jones. He had promised to buy her a share in a diamond mine situated in Nyasa Land and operated by his brother. A fabulous return was promised on the money invested. But once in possession of these funds Godfrey was seen no more.

'The man who called himself Godfrey Jones is in fact. Arthur Harold Seward, alias Godfrey Jones, alias Harold Smith. He makes a good living out of tricking ladies by lying to them. He poses as a sailor and times his arrivals and departures to the arrivals and departures of ships from the Orient and beyond.'

The rather attractive aquiline features of the young lady crumpled as her eyes closed and her cheeks reddened. She bravely tried to suppress her grief, but could not refrain from sobbing, the tears streamed readily down her cheeks in two ribbons of moisture. It was a sight to melt the most obdurate of hearts. I handed her my handkerchief with which she tried to staunch the flow of this most natural effusion of grief.

Holmes had retreated and was now donning his cloak in readiness to go out. So I was left to speak some words of comfort to the departing young lady.

'Write your home address and your employer's address on this piece of paper for Mr Holmes's records, and return to Manchester my dear. There are people who truly care for you there. I know it is difficult for you now but in a very few weeks you will be able to put this unfortunate incident behind you and look forward to a promising future as a governess.'

'That will be three guineas, by the way.' said Holmes before the lady could leave the room. 'But as Doctor Watson and I are going out we shall accompany you.' He solemnly took the three sovereigns and three silver shillings that she handed him and placed the money in his waistcoat pocket. Then going to his desk wrote her a receipt for the sum. But the generous side of Holmes's nature soon re-asserted itself, for the three of us had not progressed far down Baker Street before he hailed a Hansom Cab. He gave the driver the two of the shillings that the girl had paid him and directed that Miss Lawson be taken straight to Euston Station where she should be in time to board the 1500 train leaving platform 5 to Manchester.

We continued on our way after taking leave of Miss Lawson. He indicated that we were heading to Limehouse, but that we needed to call somewhere else first.

'I am surprised that you accepted a fee from that girl, Holmes. I doubt if you'll be able to trace that villain Seward and even if you do there will be no money at the end of the quest.'

He smiled. 'You'd be surprised to hear then my dear Watson that I actually know the precise whereabouts of this character and further when I make his acquaintance it will cost him at least 200 guineas, which will be a fair return to send on to Miss Lawson for her three guinea fee. Or at least a better profit than could be derived from any mythical diamond mine.'

I complained that the distance to Limehouse was rather excessive as the Gilzail bullet I took in Afghanistan had been giving me some pain in the last few days. 'Nonsense Watson, a brisk walk will do you a great deal of good. That wife of yours is feeding you too well and you are obviously not getting sufficient exercise, shut up all day in your consulting room. Anyway we need to attend the premises of the late Mr Zhang Wei.'

He continued striding out in the direction of the City, as if I had not spoken. We strode on in silence to the slums of the Mile End Road, but just outside a particularly squalid looking tenement we came to a halt. Holmes darted down a narrow alley and I followed him with alacrity. I nearly lost him as he took an abrupt turn to the left into a dank back yard and from thence up some stone steps. He paused in the dark doorway and producing a key opened the door that led into a cramped back kitchen, then it was a case of rounding the corner and climbing the creaking stairs two at a time.

An old woman of the working classes was seated on a chair in the space at the top of the stairs. She had a towel wrapped around her head. He expression extremely dolorous.

Holmes paused, 'Teeth bad again Mrs Grenfell?'

'Terrible Mr Holmes, terrible. Why did the good lord inflict the ooman race with such miserable items what is so obstroculous?'

'Here's a sovereign for you my dear, Oil of Clove and a few drops of Laudanum should do the trick, but you really must leave the barley sugar sticks alone.'

'Oh Mr Holmes you is a proper gent, I always said so.' chortled the old wretch whose mood was considerably improved by this windfall. Raising herself with difficulty she began to slowly descend the stairs.

Holmes took out another key which opened the door to a bedroom that stood towards the rear of the hovel. It was a most peculiar room for it contained nothing but a table with a mirror, some cupboards, a couple of wooden chairs and an adjacent oil lamp such as is used by actors and other such ruffians. The table was covered in make up jars of various hues of creams to darken or lighten the countenance. A box marked 'Beards and moustaches' also lay on the surface. Most of the rest of the space was taken up by racks of clothing and different types of boots and shoes, while on shelves situated above the racks there lay multiple hat boxes. On stands shaped like heads at various places in the room were about a dozen wigs.

'Take a seat for a moment my good chap' he said and then busily began to gather an assortment of clothes on one arm. 'Put these on and let's see how you look.'

With a certain amount of reluctance I climbed into the clothes that he wished me to wear. This was not the first time that he had required me to don a novelty outfit, and it turned out not to be the last - but I digress. Meanwhile Holmes, working like a dervish which he always did while engaged on activities he regarded as supplementary to the main purpose was throwing off his normal costume and putting on a new more disreputable one with great zest.

Since I had completed my 'transformation' more speedily I stood waiting for him to finish dressing. When he did so he seized my shoulders and twirled me around a couple of times.

24

'Military build still, Watson! You have kept yourself in good shape. It is rare to find a medical man who can follow his own advice. Just let me daub some of this paint on your face, and pop this wig on your head, they look dirty but they're not.' He applied the gunk then stood back so I could view myself in the long mirror on the wall.

I saw an older copy of myself resplendent in a rather battered version of the uniform of a Colour Sergeant of the Connaught Rangers. My general appearance spoke of sleeping rough for a few nights and a turbulent relationship with soap and hot water. 'Good lord, Holmes I can't go out like this.'

'Nonsense!,' he said, 'Compared to many of the denizens in the streets of the good Empress's capital you look quite respectable.'

'My preparations will take up quite some time, but we may as well make sure that you are up to the mark what?'

Holmes continued, 'What we will do is to mount a two pronged attack, which you will understand well considering your background in the military, just hold still - ' here he applied a little more of the obnoxious grey material from the jar. 'Oh! And one final detail, take off the jacket . . . . that's right, now put it on with only one arm in the sleeve . . the left arm. . . . I shall pin up the other sleeve.' He stood back to admire the overall effect, ' And there we have - the one armed old soldier.'

Opening a drawer in the old dresser he took out a revolver
and handed it to me with gravity. 'there is a sling to hold
it inside the jacket. Better safe than sorry!'

Back on the street in my novelty outfit I set off alone. I
soon found myself in a labyrinth of back alleys, charged
with a complex mission, the main detail of which was to
obtain entrance to an Opium den in Limehouse. The great
detective said he would see me later in the day, to do my
best, but leave the rest to him.

It was not unlike Sherlock Holmes to be vague about
details, but as I wandered towards Whitechapel I believed
that I had the gist of what was required so therefore made
my way to the public house known as the Eagle and
Child.

The problem with wearing a wig is that one is always
thinking that the thing will slip, as I entered the smokey
interior of the pub I had to restrain myself from touching
my head. However I did screw down the Glengarry a bit
firmer to hold the wig in place better. The air was hardly
breathable. In my opinion only the discharge of much
gunpowder in a confined space can produce as much
black smoke as the smoking of thick twist tobacco
(nacreous gloom?)

The old place was packed to the rafters with a varied
bunch, the odd respectable man seeking an adventure,
groups of furtive looking characters crouching over the
small metal tables with the heads together no doubt

planning crimes. Then There was a group of the ladies of the night giggling together between nervous glances towards the more prosperous characters which were their prey. But I had a specific task to fulfil and had no time for idle speculations of this type.

The landlord, portly with a wall eye, as he had been described by Holmes, served me himself. I ordered a glass of rum grog so as to stay in character.

I signalled to him that I had private message to deliver so he leaned over the bar placing his left ear near to my lips. 'I has this 'ere note what has to be given to this geezer who calls hisself Steward or Sewart or some such. There's a harf crown for you wrapped up in it, if you can see your way to givin it to 'im.'

'Small feller, bit of dandy, fancies his self?' enquired the landlord.

'Yeah! That's him. Stayin 'ere, first floor back. I was told?'

'He regarded me with the wall eye for a second. ' - and I has to give him this 'ere note?'

'Yeah, and I'm to wait for a reply, beggin your pardon for the imperance,' said I touching my Glengarry. Just at that point somebody jostled me from behind, causing me to swivel around rapidly. This precipitate action has the effect of dislodging my wig from its moorings. As I

hastily adjusted it I happened to catch a glimpse of myself
in the mirror at the back of the bar. 'Most ill favoured,' I
thought but hardly out of keeping with some of the other
ugly specimens of humanity that were haunting the place.

The large hulking chap who had disturbed my equilibrium
had now slid past me and was standing at the bar. The
landlord was still missing on his errand so he caught the
attention of the little blonde barmaid. She served him with
the pint of beer that he ordered and then he took a huge
swig consuming half the contents in one go. He sighed
and wiped the foam from his mouth. 'I needed that.' then
indicating my empty sleeve and fixing me with a gimlet
eye, 'Afghanistan?' he said.

'Yes, Gilzail bullet from a pesky Pathan, wound infected,
MO says it's the arm or your life, take your choice.'

'Bad do though. Losin' your right un.' he mused, 'Was
you ever up in Kandahar I wonder?' Soon I and this man
who had served in that unfortunate place himself were
wrapped up in a welter of memories of our times serving
the Queen in the heat and mountains of the Hindu Kush.
By this time my drink had arrived , rapidly consumed and
another ordered, treating my new friend to a pint of
whatever swill he was consuming, so I hardly noticed the
smallish fair haired gent who came from around the
corner of the bar from 'best' side and was making his way
rapidly towards me. He rudely pulled at my empty sleeve
to obtain my full attention and addressed me as follows.

'The landlord tells me that you gave him this note, to be delivered to me.' Here he brandished the item under my nose.
'What I want to know is, who was the gent that asked you to deliver it for him?' The small fair man seemed to be extremely agitated.

I took up the glass of rum grog from the bar and sipped a little of its steaming contents and mused for a second or two. 'Now lets me think. I has a terrible memory for names and faces, but I never forget a battle or a place I was stationed.' I had addressed these remarks to no one in particular but then I turned to face the small man who was wearing a short tweed jacket, peg top trousers and spats on his feet. I thought the red velvet waistcoat he sported was a trifle vulgar. 'But if my memory was to be 'elped along a bit it might work a bit better, if you takes my meaning?' In response to this statement the man put down a half sovereign on the bar top in front of me.

'Coombes, was his name.' I stated confidently.

'Are you sure that it was not Holmes?' he asked.

'That's right,' says I, 'Mr Shylock Coombes.'

The complexion of the small flashily dressed man suddenly turned very pale, no doubt arising from the sudden drop in his blood pressure due to the effusion of a stimulant by the adrenal glands. The landlord rapidly supplied him with a large brandy which he rapidly drank.

Of course I had read the message that Holmes had asked me to deliver. It was very short and to the point and read as follows.

Seward,

I have an excellent tin bath for sale. Price 200 guineas.

Yours

A well wisher

Matters proceeded apace after that and I soon found myself back on the street with no less that 220 guineas in my pocket and a note addressed to Sherlock Holmes which read.

Mr Holmes

I beg to inform you that your suppositions are incorrect. Mrs Amelia Seward, on our honeymoon in Bournemouth happened to have a fit whilst bathing, knocked her head against the bath and drowned in the bath water whilst unconscious. I had nothing to do with her death. I have entrusted a sum of money to this messenger as a token of my good faith for your trouble in looking into the affair.

G Seward

I came to the rapid conclusion on reading the note that Holmes knew a great deal more than was comfortable about this villain that preyed so wickedly on young women.

The liquor consumed had put a spring in my step, so I soon found myself in the environs of China Town. Again I set myself the task of following Holmes's instructions to the letter.

The place where the burglary and unusual murder had taken place was was a squalid four storey part dwelling house, part warehouse. Situated close to a narrow canal which smelled as if all the ordure of London was daily emptied into it.
I knocked loudly on the door and after a short pause belaboured the door again. As these efforts produced no results I began tapping on the windows and shouting, 'Open up!' 'Hello there!' 'Is there anyone in?' and similar whimsicalities. I kept this noise up for some five minutes, quite skinning my knuckles in the process as I went back and forth between windows and door treating both to many slaps and punches. My efforts were eventually rewarded when the door abruptly opened.

There, framed in the doorway, stood a young Chinese maid. She looked at me quite placidly. In the same position I would have been very angry.

'Yes?'

'I am looking to buy Jade, anything made of Jade, particularly Jade statues.' I extemporised.

'You wait there.' said she, and disappeared behind the door. After a minute or two her place was taken by a young Chinese gent who solemnly bade me enter the premises. The interior consisted of a well swept wooden floor and plain plaster walls, giving the impression of cleanliness and order. As I followed him the hall gave way to a long corridor and up to a flight of stairs, again all the floors and stairs were innocent of carpets or any other type of covering and appeared to be scrupulously clean. Ushered into a well stocked show room where I saw many glass cases containing a wealth of Chinese goods.

Here were statues of traditional Chinese gods painted in the most garish colours. There were some smaller statues showing Confucius, at least I thought them to be of him. Also a plethora of Joss Sticks, incense burners, smiling Buddhas, and rolls of rich woven materials, mainly of scarlet threaded with gold yarn. Some of the stronger looking locked cases contained intricately carved Ivory figures and some pieces of Amber in which were trapped primordial insects. I made a great display of examining the glass cases although given my attire I hardly cut the typical figure of a Western expert on Chinese cultural artefacts, but I determined to follow Holmes's instructions to the letter. The Chinese gentleman remained standing behind me impassively as I continued to study the contents of the cases.

'My employer Mr Wong, sends his compliments to the House of Zhang and also wishes me to express on his behalf condolences on the loss of your esteemed father.' I recited this as though I had learned it parrot fashion.

The man smiled and nodded.

'Mr Wong also ventures to hope that the current injustice concerning your esteemed elder brother will soon be resolved to the pleased satisfaction of all concerned.'

The man, betraying no impatience in this lengthy preamble, merely broadened his smile and gave a slight bow.

'Can I take it that I am currently enjoying the inestimable pleasure of being in the company of Mr Zhang Wu Tzu, younger brother of Mr Zhang Wu Sun who is currently incarcerated under the unjust suspicion that he murdered Old Mr Zhang?'

'Yes, I am the second son of the late Zhang Wu Chin. Your solicitude concerning the affairs of this unworthy family is much appreciated, but my worthless younger sister did chance to inform me that you were interested in the purchase of some Jade?'

I began again. 'My esteemed employer Mr Wong, whom as you know is a rival importer of Chinese goods, has instructed me to warn you regarding the quality of some Chrysolite statuettes,' here I pointed to one on a stand which was similar to the earlier statue I had seen in Holmes's rooms. The benign smile suddenly left the face of the Chinaman. I began again. 'Mr Wong is so kind as to entrust the odd errand to this poor soldier and also to reveal to him certain secrets regarding a certain secret society to which both you and he may be aware of-'

'What is wrong with the Chrysolite?' he interrupted. 'and what is this about the society?' By which he meant either the Tong or the Triad which were both secret societies of criminals greatly feared by the Chinese.

'Alas! Although I am much in the confidence of Mr Wong he did not see fit on this occasion to entrust me with the full import of his message. Instead he gave me this piece of paper on which are drawn six lines. He said that you would understand its import.

Here I produced from a grubby pocket the piece of paper upon which Mr Sherlock Holmes had drawn the six lines, which looked like this

```
———————    ———————
———————————————————
———————    ———————
———————————————————
———————    ———————
———————————————————
```

I discovered later that according to the I Ching, a Chinese fortune telling book, that this is a most unfortunate Hexagram called in their language K'an, signifying 'The Perilous Pit' in which action is required to avert great danger is indicated.

The man immediately opened a drawer in a small bureau, pulling out a well thumbed volume he studied it intently to check out the symbol and its meaning.

Shutting up the book he turned back to me with his features once again composed into a benign smile, resembling that of a Poker player determined to bluff it out to the last bet. 'Your esteemed employer Mr Wong Fu Tzu must be a most wise and honourable man, however I can assure you that his apprehensions on our behalf are groundless. Now perhaps unless you wish to make a purchase or have something else to discuss you will have no objection if this unworthy soul returns to the comfort of his humble hearth, as I am sure that there are other places more worthy of your celestial presence than this poorly stocked warehouse?'

It was obvious that my message had rattled the younger Shang but he had only let the mask slip for a second.

'It was most kind of you to spare me some of your valuable time and I will certainly pass on your good wishes to my worthy employer Mr Wong.' I was shown out with great dispatch and once more found myself back in the street, but it was now time to put the third part of Sherlock Holmes's plan into action.

With his usual vagueness he had told me to make my way into an infamous Opium Den in the close vicinity of Shang's warehouse. 'Get in, make yourself comfortable and await developments,' were his instructions, to which he had added,'BUT KEEP YOUR WITS ABOUT YOU.'

How does one conducts oneself in an opium den? I thought of myself as a respectable chap, belonging to a good profession. Doctors did not, on the whole, consort with known criminals in low public houses, or deliver cryptic messages to devious orientals, nor decidedly, did they visit opium dens in order to administer doses of noxious drugs to themselves. I must admit that I had to nerve myself, even dressed as I was, for it would be a stain even on an assumed British uniform for it to be seen entering such a place, never mind the damage the premises could do to my professional reputation as a doctor if I were to be seen entering them.

I was admitted without inquiry by an old impossibly thin Chinese lady. The place stood at the bottom of a very

narrow and dirty back alley some 200 yards closer to the
Thames than the warehouse I had just left. Fronting the
dive was a small shop selling all kinds of outlandish
Chinese sweetmeats. I rapidly passed through there and on
climbing some stairs found myself in a large space that
was given over entirely to the consumption of this vile
drug. It must have been fully fifty yards long by a cricket
pitch wide the floor being covered in mattresses on which
lay the many recumbent bodies of the poor addicts. The
only illumination in this Stygian space was due to the
small candles used to ignite the balls of opium prior to
inhaling the fumes created through the pipe. Each mattress
was provided with such a candle on a saucer for the use of
the addict.

The woman had dogged my footsteps so far, she dug a
sharp finger into my back so that I turned towards her.
'How many pipe you want?' she asked. Swiftly equating
them to drops of laudanum I said 'Oh about forty.'

Her laugh sounded like the shriek of a bird of prey
alighting on a victim, 'Heeee Heeee. He say forty pipe.
Forty pipe means dead.'

I revised my calculation to pints of Porter. 'Well say five
then.'

'Five cost you five shilling! You have money? You pay?'
I dispensed the silver shillings into her hand. 'You go
now. You lie down. I come with pipe.'

I laid myself down on the first empty mattress that I could find. I looked around me at my nearest neighbours curious to know what sort of people indulged in this vicious habit. Four men and one woman were close enough to make out. The woman appeared to be English, judging by her features and apparel, she was of middle years and strikingly handsome if not pretty. In other circumstances I would have made some excuse to have the opportunity of addressing her. Her face was oddly familiar. Our eyes happened to meet as I scrutinised her but no gleam of recognition took place. She was furiously engaged in puffing on a pipe held over a glowing ball of opium, I could see the remnants of other bits of the substance discarded on the saucer. I classified her as an addict from the smallness of the effect that the drug seemed to be having on her.

The others nearest to me were all men and fast asleep from the effects of the drug. Farther off I could discern some older Chinese from their black clothes and whiskered chins with those thin beards they often sported. My examination of the room was cut short by the arrival of two new customers both young, male and Chinese and soon by the bustling little old lady who had taken my money.

I began to feel extremely nervous. The newcomers were regarding me with undisguised hostility, a small ragged man was suddenly taking far too much interest in me, and then there was that maddeningly familiar woman who was in the act of smoking a fourth (?) pipe. She, although inhaling deeply, had her eyes fixed upon me. In the meantime the little woman had left me a lit candle on a saucer together with the pipe and five small hard balls of the opium resin.

To avoid further suspicion I essayed to begin smoking, or at least to provide the appearance of smoking because I was very reluctant to go ahead with this process. As a physician I was able to calculated to a nicety the correct dose of laudanum for the relief of a headache or the number of drams of paregoric required for an upset stomach, but the exact effect of of the vapour produced by the burning of opium was a mystery to me. I held the tiny pearl of opium in the candle flame with the tongs provided until it caught fire and began to smoke. I then dropped it quickly into the bowl of the long curved opium pipe and gave a cautious suck on the mouthpiece to breath in what I hoped was a small quantity of the vapours.

The sensation was a thousand times worse than any other intoxication that I have ever encountered. The nearest thing I ever again came to that state was on Mafeking Night a few years later. The room began to turn upside down and sway backwards and forwards, and my stomach was intent on the same evolutions that are consequent on the drinking of around ten bottles of vintage Port. Surely this could not be the effects of a mere whiff of the tail of the dragon? The prescription of another opiate such as laudanum of many drops could not possibly produce these same nauseous symptoms? I suspected that I had been deliberately given a foreign substance of a more noxious nature than the opium that the others were smoking.

My limbs had lost their purpose and flopped uselessly when I attempted to rise. My head floated like some monstrous balloon bobbing in a malign breeze. The pipe had dropped from my lips as I swooned and lay back supine on the filthy palliase, but then I was dimly aware of a close presence in that terrible place. It was the fine looking woman. She had risen from her couch and now kneeled near my head.

Help had arrived. I thought that she would no doubt arrange for my transport to the fresher air outside, and for the administration of some restorative stimulant to counter act the narcotic effects of the drug I had ingested. But to my horror she merely cradled my head in the crook of her arm, and brought the foul pipe that I had dropped back towards my lips. She placed her fingers to pinch my nose so that I was, in my pathetic state, obliged to breathe in more of those foul vapours. The noxious substance still burnt and gave off its toxic vapours. The lack of air from any other quarter resulted in my taking in huge draughts of this poison into my lungs. I barely discerned that this ambidextrous virago while she held my head in position with one arm, the hand of which closed off my nasal passage, her other hand was preparing another deadly dose in the candle flame. In one central part of my being I sensed that my end had come at last. My life's long adventure was reaching its terminus.

As you may remember I had been elaborately disguised by my friend Holmes as a one armed soldier. He had also thought to provide me with a gun in the form of a six chambered standard Remington 0.38 calibre revolver. I was dimly aware that the hand of my 'missing' arm lay close to where the gun was holstered. Only by mastering every scintilla of my crumbling will was I able to motivate myself to move this hand from its resting position.

I had lost touch with reality by this stage as I distinctly remember the dream that haunted my awareness just then where I was lost in an unfamiliar house filled with poisonous gas. To escape I had to find my way to the front door and once there operate the latch with my finger. But where was the door? Was I upstairs? downstairs? or even in the attic or cellar? I did not know. Perhaps the dream echoed the reality of my situation? But try as I may and wander where I would, the location of the door remained a mystery until in one flash of insight I realised that the door was quite close, but even then I had great difficulty in bringing up my hand to operate the latch, so that I could escape out of this miasma into the blessed outside and fill my lungs with pure air.

All this time, which seemed to stretch for hours at the time, but must have only occupied a very few seconds my other hand was endeavouring to reach the trigger of the gun. With one last burst of my rapidly declining life force I managed to find it, place my finger around it, and finally depress the trigger.

The blast of the explosion caused by the round in that quiet evil place was indeed extremely loud. The noise seemed ear shattering. In an instant the clouds of poisonous gas had parted I had found the door and operated the latch and was now outside, this sensation was rapidly followed by a true awareness of my situation. I was out of my dream awake lying on a palliase and wounded by my own shot but even so it was an extremely well aimed if random bullet. For although it had dug a track through the skin of my stomach, burnt me with the flash it had then fortuitously travelled through the arm of this female who was trying to do away with me.

Surprised by the shot she had sprung to her feet and away from me. I doubt that she was aware of her wound at that time. I managed to climb drunkenly to my feet trying to keep the revolver pointing at her. The pain from the wound in my stomach had the effect of keeping away the clouds of Morpheus which otherwise may have drawn me back to a deadly slumber.

Still smiling as if to placate me, she backed away. I could see the blood leaching from her arm.

'Stay there, stay there or by God I will kill you,' I said to her.

A faint voice was heard some distance away among the many now roused opium fiends. 'Watson. Watson, is that you?'

Keeping the gun pointed at her I shouted. 'Holmes I can't see you. It's too dark in this dreadful place, but keep calling and I will find you.'

So I stumbled around in that hideous hell hole over the recumbent forms of the addicts, many of whom had not been awakened even by the loud shot, until I saw Holmes lying in a corner his disguise perfect as a Chinaman complete with a black pig tail. But this was a very weak version of my friend even on the point of expiring. I wondered whether 'she' had attended to him in the same way as she had sought to destroy me? Or perhaps she had resolved to kill me first?

'Try and get up. Here take my arm.' Holmes rolled over onto his front, but had no strength in his arms or legs so could not rise to his feet. I grasped him under his shoulder pit and hoisted him up.

But by now forces were being assembled against us. Several of the creatures had risen to their feet and two more had climbed the stairs. The party thus assembled was blocking our way out down to the ground floor. A shot rang out closely followed by a thrown dagger that missed my face by a couple of inches. I realised with my scattered senses that I had fired the shot for one of the figures opposing us had dropped to the floor. By now Holmes had taken out his own gun. He aimed at the ceiling above the group. His bullet brought down a black shower of soot and dusty plaster on their heads. I fired at

random into the crowd who were nerving themselves to
rush us.

The men bravely stood their ground but behind them I
could spot the flurry of a skirt. 'Shoot her Watson! Shoot
her,' his own aim was obscured by the group of men. I
squeezed off another round and missed by a mile.
Suddenly a window light in the attic had been opened, the
place was filled with life giving air but our quarry had
escaped. As we in turn watched and stood, the party
melted away some through the window light but most of
them rattled down the stairs and out. In the background
we could hear the welcome sound of Police Whistles
being blown as several members of the constabulary were
no doubt rushing to where the sound of gun fire had
originated.

'It was she Watson. The woman.'

'Not Irene Adler,' I gasped. 'Surely she would not try to
kill you?'

'She was too much for me before, perhaps she wanted
another match of wits?'

'I did hear that she fell badly from grace after that affair
with the King of Bohemia. She has been seen in the
vicinity of a few recent deaths of prominent public figures
or so I heard.'

'You don't mean -' I gasped, 'that she has become an assassin?'

'My heart was filled with pity when I saw her lying on one of those dreadful mattresses, a beautiful creature of such resource, but I realise now that I fell right into her trap. Don't forget Watson that there is a price on my head. I do wonder if Professor Moriarty is at the back of it? But I suppose we shall never know.'

'Come let us get out of here.' Holmes was in a much worse case than me but somehow I got him down the stairs but he had to lie down on the pavement once we reached it. I had not realised during all the excitement that I myself had been bleeding profusely for my outfit was soaked in blood from my wound.

The police arrived. Fortunately our friend Mr Gregson was the officer in charge rather than that buffoon Lestrade. They brought up a couple of tables to use as stretchers and wrapped us both in blankets before carrying us to the Black Maria where the two horses clip clopped us to the station where a police surgeon had been alerted to care for us. He placed no less than ten stitches in my flesh wound after swabbing the area with Iodine. I must say that the hot sweet tea laced with rum was more beneficial to my spirits than the stitches, but it is always hard for a surgeon to take his own medicine for I had stitched up enough similar wounds in my time as a Medical Officer in Afghanistan.

Holmes came to himself after the application of some Sal Volatile and started to take an interest in what was going on in the station around us. At one point Mr Zhang Wu Tzu was led into the station the man I had interviewed back at the warehouse earlier on. Inspector Lestrade, looking incredibly smug as he arrived at the station, had made the arrest shortly after the fracas at the opium den. We asked the constables and their supervisors about 'the Woman' but of her there was no trace.

They brought us both a Corned Beef sandwich each and a mug of hot cocoa. Most of the constables knew Holmes personally and not a few of them had been grateful for his help to their families in times of distress, so we were more than welcome to all the amenities the station had to offer.

I was confused about the arrest of the younger brother Zhang when the elder had originally been charged with the crime of his father's murder.

'It is quite simple Watson. Wu Tzu murdered his father and arranged things to make it look like his elder brother had committed the crime.'

'But how Holmes? Was not the late Mr Zhang found with fatal head injuries in a locked and barred room? That can't be very easy to explain.'

After taking a long sip of his cocoa, Holmes studied the mug for a moment. 'You are quite correct Watson for until the events of the last few hours it was very hard to explain, but just imagine the consequences upon the constitution of a feeble old gentleman of smoking some of that deadly substance that nearly did for us? Amanita Phalloides by the way, one of the most poisonous substances in the world, yet a common enough mushroom in our woods and coppices.'

We were interrupted by the reappearance of the young police surgeon who wanted to have another look at my stomach wound.

'Makes a nice change from dead bodies. I had nearly forgotten how to suture a wound.' he confessed. I told him he had done a good job.

Then with the help of three policemen and the useful Black Maria we were taken back to Mrs Hudson's lodgings where they insisted on chairing us both up the stairs to Holmes's rooms. I spent the night and the next few nights in my old bed in his rooms. Shock set in for us both but Mrs Hudson and my, speedily returned, wife Mary shared the nursing duties to an admirable extent. It took us both some days to recover from the nausea brought about by the poisoning. As a medical man I knew that the Opium we had been given was super refined to induce quick loss of consciousness, but that the toxins in the 'Death Cap' mushrooms would take days to destroy our liver and kidney functions.

There were several points about the case that excited my curiosity but it had to wait over a week before the full facts of the cases emerged. I was propped up in bed enjoying a second breakfast cup of tea. Holmes was sitting in an easy chair near my bed. The women were in conference about better ways to immobilise us both and delay our return to normal duties. Whereas we were both determined to be back on our feet within another couple of days.

'What were we doing in that dreadful Opium Den Holmes?'

'Ah! That went a bit wrong. I was expecting Wu Tzu to arrive because he had been spending too much money there and I also wanted to make a note of his partners in crime. But he never turned up and as they say – the rest is history. I wanted you there as a back up in case of trouble. And to be frank Watson you did splendidly, but for you that would have been the end of me.'

'Oh don't mention it Holmes, you have done the same for me on more than one occasion. But I still don't follow how young Wu Tzu did away with Mr Zhang?'

'This is how it happened to the best of my knowledge. On the evening of his demise old Mr Zhang was examining the Jade statuette and smoking his last ever pipe, which had been poisoned by his youngest son with some of the strong Opium, When Shang fell to the ground Wu Tzu took the statuette from his poor father's hands and proceeded to beat the old man about the head with it until he died. The great feature being that with the old man unconscious there was no noise. The young man had taken the precaution of locking the door first from the inside. Then all he had to do was to lift a few previously loosened floor boards and hide underneath the floor until the next morning. It was a simple matter of waiting his chance, then during the ensuing hullabaloo on the discovery of the body he swiftly emerged from his hiding place and pretended to have just arrived, as if he had just come down the stairs from his bedroom. In the process he gave the impression of being the last on the scene and diverted suspicion away from himself.'

'How did you know this Holmes?'

Holmes got up and pulled his chair closer to the side of my bed and tapped the side of his nose. It was only a theory but I told the good Inspector Lestrade to use his nose when he went back to the crime scene.'

'I still don't understand,' I said

'The English are not the only race addicted to the excessive drinking of tea,' he said casting a glance in the direction of my huge breakfast cup.'

The light dawned on my feeble intellect.

'Ah I see and the young man was trapped under the floor for over eight hours after drinking lots of Souchong Tea.'

'And tea,' Holmes added, 'is a diuretic.'

*** *** ***

Stories we get stuck with

Being a reflection on convictions

Having less libido than usual due to a bout of the flu, I
chanced to play an old recording of the Mussorgsky Opera
'Khovanshchina' and this threw me into an interesting
speculation about causes and mindsets that stays with me
as I write these words. The action of the opera is set
towards the end of the 17th century in Moscow, when
several conflicting movements come to a head. The
character Khovanski is a boyar or nobleman, who led, or
inspired, a revolt against the tsar. His group were known
as the Streltsi and included many Old Believers who,
opposed as they were to religious reforms, found common
cause with Khovanski's followers.

Current at the same time were certain changes to the
liturgy of the Russian Orthodox Church which were
brought about in a spirit of 'modernism' to make it more
compliant and similar to the Greek Orthodoxy. The head

cleric in Moscow was a man called Nikon, and it was he
that persuaded the tsar to approve these reforms. This led
to a great deal of trouble, because many worshippers
found the change of words to be unacceptable to their
interpretation of the faith. These dissidents were
thenceforward referred to as 'Old Believers'.

 A very similar thing happened in the Church of England
in the 1970's when it was decided to modernise the
wording of the services away from the Book of Common
Prayer which had held sway for the last three hundred
years. The effect of these changes into such inferior
English was to render the whole service meaningless to
me, and any comfort or spirituality I may have once
experienced, was swept away as if in a tide of ordure. You
may point out here that the matter is one of mere
semantics or even symbolism or semiotics, but that is
rather the point of these few paragraphs that will be
developed lower down.

Eventually the Old Believers were first excommunicated,
and then persecuted for their beliefs, or more accurately,
their refusal to adapt them to the modern sensibilities.
Then the most peculiar notion took hold amongst them,
that of 'Baptism by Fire'. In the year 1676 upwards of ten
thousand of these souls committed suicide by mass
immolation. They believed that, if they were to die in this

awful manner, that their souls would be redeemed from any sin resulting from their banishment and be immediately accepted into heaven, and passed through the pearly gates. In the years that followed, many more were to die in this way. Some opted to have their heads cut off, and others to be buried alive – the mind rather boggles at these excesses. The only modern example of mass suicide that comes to mind is the infamous business of Jones-Town, something that still makes me shudder. Where a group of American Communist zealots were persuaded to commit mass suicide. With the exception of the twin towers, Jones-Town remains the largest murder/suicide of American citizens (918) in recorded history.

As I was researching these terrible things the concept of 'being stuck with a story' came into my mind, and a word in the Mussorgsky opera set off other bells ringing in my head. The Old Believers were referred to in the Russian Language as 'Raskolniks' which means either 'Schismatics' or 'Cleavers'. The reason this word made me want to metaphorically 'reach for my gun' was that Raskolnikov is the anti-hero of Dostoevsky's great novel 'Crime and Punishment'. Why should this great author have used the name of this fairly obscure group of people as that of his central and probably greatest character?

53

The reason is, that like the Old Believers, Raskolnikov has been 'stuck with a story'. In his case the story is, that the end justifies the means. Down on his luck as an impoverished student in the Moscow of 1890 odd, he reads a, probably fictitious, account of how, the then young, Napoleon steals some money. Then with the proceeds of this crime Napoleon escapes from poverty in Corsica and re-invents himself as a soldier in France before then aspiring to his destiny of greatness. In the novel this mistaken idea, of how to become great, leads to Raskolnikov, in a most bloodthirsty manner, murdering an old money lender and her daughter with an axe. He steals their gold, which he then buries. Rather than profiting from this appalling crime he then drifts in introspection. It is the process by which he comes to examine and reject this 'story' that leads to his redemption via the admission of his guilt and the acceptance of the just punishment that follows.

I think that we all get stuck with stories, narratives that somehow explain or excuse our past. If the stories are not narratives they probably take the form of 'great ideas' or 'obsessions', be they religious or political, that drive our sensibilities and either open doors or close them in our path. Misery loves company and we tend to soon locate others suffering from similar delusions, with whom we immediately identify, often to the exclusion of people we have known since childhood, thus becoming ever more divorced from reality. In my experience, these sort of

liaisons, based on mutual delusions, rarely end well.
Several times in my life I have been seduced by such
stories, and I have always looked back on these episodes
with a feeling of shame. Without a grain or two of self
respect or basic caution these 'stories we are stuck with'
can often ruin our lives or make the way forward more
difficult than it should be.

Life is all about probability. There is nothing that is clear
cut. Randomness rules. If you have done well, the chances
are that you have been lucky. Even those who try their
best often do not succeed, or sometimes even manage to
get by. On average 'trying your best' is a recipe for a
mundane but secure existence, anything else is a bonus.
To be influenced by some internal nonsensical narrative is
the epitome of irrationality. The truth is, that the future
course of events, is perfectly random and will not be
influenced by either your prayers or convictions.

It is not the role of these few words to do more than
indicate how these heuristics can be remedied, for we all
cherish our own delusions dearly. There would not be
space in a hundred pages to set down my own silly
notions. Recent reading of the works of Daniel Kahneman
and Nassim Nicholas Taleb, not to mention Karl Popper,
does indicate one fairly simple notion which paradoxically
is the notion of complexity. I would say categorically
'Distrust the simple. Embrace complexity.' Any concept

that can adequately be explained in ten words or less is probably wrong. I remember the case of a Nobel Prize winning chemist who was interviewed by a journalist representing the 'Daily Dung Heap' who was asked 'Can you explain your work on Ligands simply for the benefit of our readers?' The Nobel laureate gave a one word answer 'No' he said.

So going forward remember please to distrust everything that convinces you, for it is certainly likely to be wrong, and avoid people who are convinced they have a monopoly on the truth, for they are very dangerous. Cultivate the saying 'I don't know.' and you cannot go too far wrong

Everice got lucky.

Call me Zeke, dead since this day year in 1863, July 3rd to be exact. Marching up Cemetery Ridge at Gettysburg under General Longstreet I caught a couple of minie balls in my chest and that was the end of me. Few of the men that died around me that day knew what we were supposed to be fighting for, and if you ask an old timer I reckon that there is still some doubt whether the whole shebang made any sort of sense.

One way and another when they got down to counting, sixty thousand young Americans died at Gettysburg. More than in the rest damned Civil War put together.

Ezekiel Jeremiah Doodson is my full name and I was twenty five years old, already with a wife and two children back in Virginia where I had work as a school master. So there I was alive one minute and dead the next and there sure was a parcel of confusion. I had my sergeant's stripes so 'they' whoever they are, cause to this day, I ain't a clue how this system works, 'they' decided that someone had to organise things a little.

'An orderly transition' this smart looking guy in the white suit said. I often wondered whether he was God? So I got to work sorting the wheat from the chaff, the sheep from the goats and I reckon, though I have shifted from Philadelphia to Baltimore that is the sort of work (excuse the pun) that remains before my hands to this day.

Now I am dead. There is no doubt about that, call it a certainty if you like, a simple fact. But nothing is ever that simple, as I would hope you know. Once you start thinking things are simple that is where you can go seriously wrong. Some people get used to the idea of being dead pretty quick, do what they have to do, and pass on up the ladder. Others, like me, want to hang around or something keeps them down here, or it could be they are too attached, not prepared to let go. Others go plumb crazy, start throwing things around, putting scares into the living and doing all manner of spooky stuff.

These souls have what we politely call 'adjustment problems' and there ain't much we can do to rectify matters apart from wait. My job is to comfort the newly dead, tell them that it will soon be OK, find them useful things to do and just hold the line, and keep on marching up to Cemetery Ridge. I'm an old soldier after all. Did I tell you my name is Zeke?

In this sea of confusion that we call the afterlife I come across fellow souls moving in the same direction. This coloured girl, Everice, was one of them I got to know real well. What follows is her story, or at least a small part of it.

Everice was hit and killed, by a stray bullet as she walked with her dog Lucky, to help with a siege situation that had developed in one of the project blocks we have here in Baltimore. She looked real cute in her blue outfit, it had only seemed right to have her hair dyed red to contrast, although many young bloods were none too keen on sisters with red hair in those days.

Everice was one of a service that is now called Police. She was not a policewoman, certainly not a policeman, for neither of those terms were now politically acceptable. Instead she was Police, not even the rather apologetic Police person.

In spite of all this unimportant signage Everice liked to think of herself as a 'Police lady' because it sounded more refined. Everice O Dowd, had herself been brought up in the Projects and, as was too often the case, by a single mother for her father had found the duties of paterfamilias to be so overwhelming that he got himself shot to death robbing a Korean Convenience Store when she was three.

But now his daughter, twenty five years later, had fallen victim to another bullet.

She was a big girl, but had a good figure, working out often in the free gymnasium provided for the service. Her hair fashionably kinky. She would have been 28 if she had lived another 29 days. Her childhood had been more about survival than education or nurture, but at least her mother, now also prematurely dead, had managed to at least feed and keep clean clothes on her increasing brood, gathered through a series of increasingly disastrous relationships.

Like many of her class Everice left High School without a completion certificate and had laughed openly when the well meaning teacher had mentioned SATS. Arlene, a girl she knew, a year older, had joined the army and done OK. Everice did the same. From then on she did OK too. Everything denied to her by her haphazard home life and gang dominated High School was provided in abundance by the army.

Something had tugged at her uniform as she moved up to get behind Officer Blair Wilkins who crouched behind a squad car. The random bullet had entered the right atrium of her heart. This bullet had no right to be doing anything like that. This guy, down on his luck had been firing random shots all morning from a window in his first floor apartment, until somebody decided to call the police. If the little 22 slug could have apologised it would have done so, but the damage was done. For in spite of all the fine words and good intentions that exist for the better instruction of mankind, a bullet in the heart finalises most things beautifully.

Falling to the ground she cussed silently but was soon up on her feet for Lucky, a large German Shepherd always dragged on his lead. She bent down close to Wilkins and said. 'Hi Blair, How you doin?' But Wilkins seemed too abstracted to answer her. Everice stayed in the position a little longer until a cramp started in her right leg. She always got a cramp there, for in her military service a chip of shrapnel had hit her thigh in a barricade near Kandahar. Her head suddenly felt very light as if she was going to faint. Backing off slowly she walked around the corner. Lucky thought he was going back in the van, so Everice thought she might as well load him in, which she did.

With the dog out of the way she wandered off, bemused at this sudden lack of direction. The sky had gone a funny purple colour and her vision was not quite the same as before, for now all the people she saw moving in the street had rainbow coloured fringes about them. Poor girl, she did not know for some time, but she had just entered the confusing world of the recently dead. Deciding against reporting sick she went home.

As it happened she lived a few blocks away. Everice should have taken the van with her. It was strictly against orders to leave an animal locked up in a van, but she had this funny feeling come over, you know? As if nothing mattered and to be fair, nothing would really ever matter again, in her past life that is.

Floyd her husband was at home. His wheel chair drawn up close to the TV. He was watching a re-run of the game between Alabama and Clemson. Floyd was always at home on account of him being a paraplegic on 100% disability army pension. He too had been wounded outside Kandahar but Floyd never got over his wound, a bullet fired from a well meaning Taliban man's Kalashnikov that he received in the lower spine. The Veteran's administration treated him real well. Gave him a dandy wheel chair, where all he had to do was suck or blow through this white tube and the chair would know what to do. It was just as well that he had such a doo hickey to sit in because since he was paralysed from the neck down there were not many things that Floyd could do for himself.

It could have been worse, Everice and he had been married two weeks before his injury. Two solid weeks of connubial bliss, or it would have been if both of them had not been on duty at least half the time. Again the V.A. provided a nurse who came in twice every day to change his colostomy bag and empty out his pee, but even on the days she did not show, Everice did it. 'No big deal' she said.

'Hi Floyd. I'm back. Feel sort of jittery, think I'll ring Sergeant Flynn let him know huh?'

Floyd did not reply. Everice went into the kitchen to make coffee. Floyd was probably having one of his moods, but these never bothered her for he was basically a good humoured guy, and one thing about his injuries meant that he would never walk out on her.

She joked that if he tried that she would remove the batteries from his whizzo wheelchair. For some reason she could not operate the faucet neither could she pick up the coffee pot. She shrugged and returned to a seat in front of the 75 inch television screen. Floyd's attention was fixed on the features of Nick Sabin the Alabama coach who stood on the side line wearing a Covid mask silently willing his team to win. A few more chance remarks being ignored Everice got up and waved a hand in front of Floyd's eyes temporarily blocking out the television. The man did not react. As she turned to speak again she noticed the floating head at the back of the room.

One does not often see floating heads that are not attached to a neck with a body lower down to support them. If you should happen to see such thing my advice is not to panic, for there are only two possible explanations, you are either going mad, or what you are seeing is really there. As Everice watched, frozen into immobility by the strange phenomenon, the disembodied head suddenly spoke.

'Sorry about this honey, but it's one of the best ways to get someone's attention.' Everice made out that the being addressing her was a lady possessing an elaborate blonde hairdo reminiscent of Dolly Parton, who once famously remarked that it was very expensive to look that cheap.

As Everice continued to watch the rest of the spooky figure came slowly into view.

The blonde locks fell in luxurious profusion down the back of what the police lady could see was a scantily clad figure wearing only a light blue silver lame cocktail dress and ridiculous six inch high stilettos. Finally the full figure stood before her about ten feet away at the back of the lounge.

 'You would have thought the old feet would let up some, wouldn't you honey, considering that we are where we are? Do you mind.'

The figure tottered around some more and finally sank onto the black leather sofa at the back of the room that had cost $1200 second hand and that no one ever sat on.

'What are you doin' here?' Everice asked. She had decided that whatever it was she was seeing was real and therefore it might be possible to talk to 'it'.

'Come on have a seat honey. I don't bite. Take the weight off your feet. I have some news for you and it ain't so good. Be better if you is sitting down.' Everice did as she was commanded, slowly lowering herself onto the low black sofa. 'Can't wrap it up too much for you child, things to do, places to go, but the fact is that you is dead.'

'How can I be dead. Why I am sitting here in my home, our home I mean, me and Floyd. I just came home cause I felt a bit weird, nothing too heavy. Anyway s if I was dead I would be lying somewhere, you know, going stiff, not saying much and kinda still. But that ain't so is it? Cause I'm sitting here talking to you.'

A ghostly ring encrusted hand was placed on Everice's knee. It did not feel particularly cold, it did not feel much like anything. 'I know Honey, I know believe me! You can imagine how I felt when I was just ready to go on and someone came to tell me.'

'Go on where?'

65

The large blue mascara encrusted eyes blinked. 'I'm an entertainer, child. ain't that kinda obvious?'

Catching the drift at last Everice said, 'When they came to tell you that you was dead?'

'I made a beautiful corpse. Folk just kept on sayin' "Why I can't believe Maybelline is dead" Course I was dead, there ain't no doubt about that. Something to do with my brain, Altruism?'

'Aneurysm.' said Everice. Then she suddenly brightened up, she was always like that, prone to accept the bad things and quickly make the best out of them. 'I think I know what you used to do?'

'Oh yeah,' said the other lady getting up from the sofa.

'You was a Dolly Parton tribute act.' But the other figure had again begun to fade into invisibility. This time from the ground up.

'Yeah that's right Honey but I has to go now, cause people are dying all the time and I have to get around all the ones in my zone. But listen if you need me all you have to do is hum the tune 'Jolene'. You know it?' As she said this 'Maybelline' disappeared and Everice was left alone.

After that time passed kind of slowly. Everice wandered around the small living space for a while. When she became bored with that activity she tried to get Floyd's attention. Alabama had built up a twenty five point lead and there was five minutes left in the fourth quarter, but as she watched the TV screen over Floyd's left shoulder Trevor Lawrence threw a touch down for Clemson. Floyd did not respond. She tried to touch him but he still did not respond. Touching was different she found. She could feel the surface she was touching but was unable to exert any pressure, no matter how hard she pushed. Shrugging, she returned to the black sofa and hummed 'Jolene'.

'I don't know what to do with myself. You tell me that I'm dead. I mean to say I ain't contradicting you, but what am I supposed to do? Do you have any ideas? How does it work, being dead?'

'Best thing honey is to go pick up the threads. Go back to where you was killed. Follow your body to the morgue and all that. Hang around the hospital for a bit, sooner or later something will occur to you and you can start living again.'

'Living?' Everice echoed, but the blue clad effigy of Dolly Parton had begun to disappear again. Maybelline turned out to be the purveyor of good advice for it was better to be outside and away from the close spaces of the tiny flat. She found herself standing on the exact spot where she had been shot four hours earlier.

Everice looked around nervously, this 'being dead' business was something that was going to take a parcel of getting used to and then some. She was suddenly aware of somebody standing close by. A man, a large gentleman of colour. Unlike the passers by he was not surrounded by a rainbow aura.

Although they were standing close to each other neither of them spoke. The immediate area was decorated with 'scene of crime tape', strewed with gay abandon over lamp posts and parked vehicles to inform members of the public that an unpleasant incident had taken place there.

They continued to stand in silence and Everice noticed that the man had a gun in his hand. Suddenly she knew the whole story. She turned to him. 'You shot me with that gun.'

'I can't seem to put it down, and I'se standin' out here. Everthin' going wrong sister.' He rolled his eyes piteously but drew no sympathy from the young woman.

'Why's you shoot me? I done you no wrong.'

'Everthin' goin wrong. My woman she upped and left me, and she took all the stuff. Man I had us some good crack. Man we used to free base together, whenever she got money we had ourselves a time.'

'What you usin?'

'Crank, Blow, Rocks sometimes depends what we could get you know.'

'So why you start shootin?'

'I'se told you. My woman gone, all the stuff and everthin we use, pipes, bongs you know? I needed some help? But there ain't no help for Dwayne, so he just takes his old gun out and starts shootin outta the window.'

'One of your bullets done hit me. It killed me. Right there where's you standin. And I got some news for you bro, for if you'se speakin to me now, which you is, it ain't good.'

For the first time the large man of colour thought about his situation. 'I guess I will go back upstairs and get me some rest. Maybe I'll feel OK after a while.' He turned and started to walk away. Everice walked after him. She found that going up the stairs was easy. All you had to do was just think where you wanted to go and your body just floated there.

Soon they were standing outside Dwayne's front door on the first floor. This portal too was decorated in the yellow and black scene of crime tape. Neither of them knew why the door opened, perhaps it did not open, but they found themselves standing amidst the chaos of Dwayne's flat.

A female figure was crouched on a dirty black sofa. The woman was small and extremely thin, looking like she had not washed her body or combed her hair in quite a while. Everice noticed that the sofa resembled the one in her place that was never used. This sofa however bore the traces of continuous brutal abuses as its leather was distorted, baggy and out of shape. At points the cushions were only a few inches above the floor. The floor itself was disgusting. The couple must have at one time kept a dog.

'Estrella baby, you've come back.' Dwayne cried. The woman took no notice of him. Everice knew the reason for her lack of attention but tragically Dwayne did not.

Everice had no compassion for Dwayne. The man himself crossed the untidy space and seated himself at a table near the window. Everice noticed that every splinter of glass had been removed from the window. The big window led onto to a small balcony. It was from there that the fatal shot that had killed her had been fired.

Everice looked over the woman's shoulder to see what she was doing. A small spirit burner was lit on the floor. The woman was cooking a dose of heroin to inject into her arm. The white powder lay in small pile inside a dirty blackened spoon. She (Estrella) was holding the spoon above the tiny blue flame and watching as the powder dissolved into liquid.

The ex-police lady turned away. She had a strong stomach but the sight of someone poking a dirty needle into scab filled inner elbow where the veins were all ruined, was too much even for her. Suddenly Dwayne was standing over them demanding his share of the wonderful goodness marooned in the dirty spoon.

'Why does it have to be this way?' Everice asked herself, not for the first time. The woman proceeded to stick the dirty needle into herself, depress the plunger. The man looked on disappointed that none of the contents of the syringe had come his way. 'You seen the woman in the blue dress yet, my man?'

'No I ain't seen nobody but you.'

'You will,' said Everice and floated out of the room. After that for the next few days, she never stayed anywhere too long but was here and there minutes at a time. It was real tough watching how Floyd, her husband took the news. He took it hard, but you know, there is hope even for a paraplegic, because the nurse from the VA took a fancy to him and within a couple of years they had moved in together. Everice was pleased he had found somebody else. But by then she had her own work to do because the spirit world has its necessities and what she had done before meant that she had useful skills.

Not everybody who dies hangs around. Those with full lives, that were ready, soon passed on and upwards, but for people like me, Maybelline and certainly Everice. Those of us left with a sense of incompleteness it was not easy to move on.

In the event Everice passed up the ladder pretty quickly, but she had to put some time in helping out like we all do. She got to know Maybelline after a while, but it took her a few weeks to adjust to the way things are. I told her that you always feel better after the funeral is out of the way. Soon Everice was running the station. It might have been a year it might have been twenty. Time is not the same after you die. Then she got passed up and it was back down to me and Maybelline to carry on without her. She

73

told us that last day that soon we would all be together again on the next plane. We just smiled and nodded. It is a long time since Gettysburg in my case and for Maybelline it was Nashville in 1999.

'Perhaps we is too attached to earthly things,' Maybelline said one day, 'you know with Everice making it up there so soon.'

'No it ain't that' I said, 'I think maybe she just got lucky.'

The Biscuit Barrel

Alice had gone from light blonde to silver almost
overnight, but overnight had occupied five years, only
Siobhan her hairdresser knew the full story. Alice Bradley
was seventy three but still proud of her size twelve figure
and thick hair. Standing at five feet three in her nylon
tights, she still preferred skirts to trousers, only the
addition of a pair of spikes brought her up to average
height. There were a couple of elderly eligible widowers
at her church who would have liked to get to know her a
bit better. But Alice had an air of 'no nonsense' about her
that did not encourage familiarity, even with fellow
worshippers.

Every four weeks she repaired to the small hairdressers
which stood at the bottom of Stocks Lane in a terraced
house. She had kept this regular habit up now for more
years than it was comfortable for her to remember. That
year even Siobhan was getting older. Could the young
hairdresser really be fifty? Alice wondered. By force of
habit and circumstance four women, five counting
Siobhan had been thrown together in the tiny shop,
between the hours of eleven and one on Thursday
mornings precisely four weeks apart.

There was Mary Goggins, Sixty nine and widowed like
Alice. Mary ran to fat and was always on a diet. Beryl
Siddeley a spinster of seventy. Beryl died her hair
privately and no one was supposed to know, but her
straggly Auburn locks did not convince. Barbara Burton,
another widow, brought up the quartet. Barbara was the
eldest at the age of 78 but could still get around – just. But
Barbara was also getting very forgetful, careless even, and
the other women were concerned that one night she would
not lock up, or not turn the gas off after cooking. The way
of ageing was fraught with peril, or as someone put it
'Growing old is not for wimps'. Siobhan hailed from
Northern Ireland and was very fair with skin that easily
burned in the sun. Her dexterity with her scissors was
mirrored in her conversational skills. She never had to
resort to tired old cliches to get the conversations going
without which no visit to the hairdressers can be enjoyed.
No, she knew all her client's well and what to say to
prime the pumps of feminine loquacity

Alice although a good listener was reticent about her past.
That she had once lived in Macclesfield, been married to a
chap that worked for BT and had two children by him she
never revealed. That final Thursday in November 2012
was to prove the last meeting, for Alice died on Christmas
day. Siobhan was not big on closing the shop over past
times. Sure she enjoyed being with her family, in spite of
the fact that she wished her two sons had chosen better
partners. But Christmas was all about an armistice as far
as she was concerned. She hated Tracey and had no time
for Claire, and to be honest the babies they brought with

them were not well behaved, but the average two or three year old is not privy to strict social customs, according to Siobhan toddlers must be endured rather than enjoyed. Privately Siobhan did not particularly like children.

She and Patrick, who worked in demolition had married young back in Belfast then taken the conscious decision to emigrate to England, seeing no future for themselves in that difficult province. Life in England had been hard at first and they had travelled the country for a year staying wherever Patrick could get work. With her trade as a hairdresser Siobhan could always either 'rent' a chair in a salon or even work a week or two for poor wages in any small back street hairdresser. She was happy with whatever she could earn in those days in the late eighties for it was all extra.

'So Alice is dead?' she thought to herself standing in the kitchen at around two in the afternoon of Christmas day. She was smoothing a layer of thick whipped cream onto the top of a large sherry trifle. Almost absently she poured a drop of the cheap sherry from the litre bottle into her glass. Ructions were coming from the living room, one of the children. Little Barry had trapped his fingers somewhere and was addressing his grief to the world. Soon the other one Shane would join in. Her two daughter in laws were sitting drinking white wine, their attention fixed on the large 72 inch TV screen where a video of Disney's 'Cinderella' was showing. This had been put on to entertain the babies who were, of course, oblivious to it. The two young women continued to stare at the screen with that solidity of attention that only constant exposure to crying babies will produce. A numbing of the senses that Dame Nature provides to prevent us from murdering our offspring.

'So Alice is dead?' Siobhan thought again taking another sip of the sherry. She looked at the kitchen clock where the time now stood at 1405. The men would not be back until three at the earliest, when the meal had been scheduled. The Turkey 'Crown' was roasting in the oven surrounded by roast potatoes and a tin of sage and onion stuffing. The veg, carrots, sprouts and potatoes all stood in pans on the cooker hob waiting to be boiled. A pan of Oxtail Soup also was ready to be heated. Everything else, rolls and butter, cheese and biscuits, red wine to have with the meal, stood on the table in the lounge. The Christmas pudding would heat up quickly in the microwave and the white sauce stood ready in yet another sauce pan to be heated up. Siobhan would be glad when the men got back. She loved her husband and her two sons to distraction, and thought it a pity that the boys had encumbered themselves with these two stupid English women and their obnoxious children.

'Anybody fancy a cup of tea?' she called through into the lounge. She knew that her two daughter in laws would have to remain reasonably sober to drive their respective families home after the meal.

'Ooh that will be very nice,' said Tracey without looking away from the television or offering to help. Tracey's role at work as a nurse was to help people. But this charity began and ended at work and was not practised elsewhere, particularly in the house of her mother in law.

'What about you Claire? Do you fancy a cup?' No answer. This again was pretty typical for Claire was a 'Space Cadet' as far as Siobhan was concerned. The birth of little Barry had robbed the young woman of all of her wits, and she now existed in a very modern 'Woke' consciousness, more concerned with the welfare of minorities and Social Justice than either cooking meals for her family or keeping her house clean. Claire had been to university and taken a degree in Sociology at Salford, and the marks still showed. Whatever she had learned at college being vastly inferior to the things she had forgotten.

The lady of the house made the tea, gave it to the girls. She then changed nappies on one of the babies and perching herself again in the corner of the kitchen went back to the cheap Sherry. 'So Alice is dead.' she said for the third time and thought back to the one time she had ever been alone with Alice. The Irish girl had had a scare. A small lump in her left breast that either could foretell an early death or just the inconvenience of therapy. Alice had been in the waiting room of the 'Macmillan Unit' when Siobhan had arrived for her appointment.

'Did you enjoy your holiday?' Alice asked, for Patrick had recently taken Siobhan to Greece for the first time. 'When me and Geoff went to Crete things were different then. It was in 1972. You hardly saw any tourists where we stayed.'

'I hated it. Too hot and the food didn't agree.'

'That's a shame.' commented Alice.

'I can't see any point in holidays, without children I mean. We always took the boys to a holiday camp, they loved it. Me and Patrick just fitted in around them.'

'But you were always glad to get back home?'

'Oh yes. Holidays are hard work. I think so anyway.'
After that the conversation died and soon Alice was called for her appointment, and that was the total of private conversation that Siobhan the hairdresser ever had with her client Alice. The lump in her breast was removed by Mr Brierley the general surgeon a month later, and the hairdresser made a full recovery.

Christmas had come and Christmas had gone. January 2013 was here and the three remaining old ladies had assembled for their Thursday morning appointment at the salon. The talk was a little restrained out of respect for the departed member of the quartet but soon the matter of the biscuit barrel was raised. Mary, Beryl and Barbara confessed themselves fascinated by this peculiar turn of events when Siobhan told them what had happened.

'You know I always take Mondays off. Well! It makes it more of a break with having to work Saturdays,' Saturdays were what kept the Irish hairdresser's show on the road. What she made from the old ladies that came midweek was mere pocket money. But late Friday afternoons and Saturday afternoons were a different matter. The young and not so young women that came for hairdos on these days needed to look their best. It was either a hot date on Friday evening or a night around the pubs man hunting on either night. Siobhan had even expanded into make up for an extra consideration.

'It was before I had opened up on Tuesday. Me and Margaret (Siobhan's assistant) were mopping the floor, and there was ever such a loud knock on the door. It was the postman. I was just on the point of asking him what he was playing at and why could he not put it through the letter box when I saw he was holding this huge parcel. I had to sign for it all legal and proper like. We made a cup of coffee and sat down. Well I mean our first client was not until ten thirty. The parcel had been sent from the solicitors dealing with Alice's will. There was a short letter saying that Alice had wanted it to be sent to me at the shop, and that was it really!'

'Are you sure that was all it said,' asked Beryl to whom nothing was ever straightforward.

'Oh there was one thing about how we all had to read the letter that was in the biscuit barrel then decide among ourselves what to do with it.'

'Well read it then!,' said Mary who was a trifle bossy.

The message in the biscuit barrel:-

'Well Girls when you get to read this I won't be around any more. The doctors say I have not got to worry but I know differently. I have put this note in the biscuit barrel for a reason. When you have read this you will know why.

I started with the GPO from school as a telephonist, did well and got a transfer to Macclesfield. Geoff, my husband to be, was the manager of the telephone exchange, you might remember it was all STD in those days before everything went solid state, but I won't bore you with all that. I was living in digs and so was he. He got two tickets for the Policeman's Ball asking me if I would like to go with him. He proposed to me a fortnight later. He told me that in spit of having three sisters he'd always been a bit chary of women, I told him I did not know what to do with a lad. He said we would find out together.

So there was I by 1965 living in a semi in Bollington with the two children Keith and Mildred. Geoff had got a couple of promotions and had to travel around so he was out early and back late. We only courted for a year then I fell pregnant so we brought the wedding plans forward. His mum Katie and my mum were both widows so it was not a fussy wedding, but I did have three bridesmaid for his sisters were younger than he was.

Keith was born within six months of the wedding and Mildred came along two years later. We were as happy as we could be in the circumstances what with his job and the children and so on. Those are the best years you know, the ones that you look back on with fond memories, but they are not much fun at the time.

Geoff, had a particular friend called Jim Brown. They had know each other all their lives. By coincidence Jim worked in a textile place where they did testing in Bollington, so the two men were able to keep in touch. Then Jim met Anne and fell in love with her. It seemed the most natural thing for two courting couples to go out together. So that was how it went. We were all keen on dancing, not this modern stuff. Every week it was one night at the Palais and another at the cinema all four of us. After marriage we continued to see Jim and Anne who had also tied the knot. They were living in Stockport by then. Anne had a bad time with their baby, little Christopher. He was born six weeks premature and she was always on the point of losing him all through the pregnancy. They decided not to have any more children.

I don't know how it got started, the business with the barrel. It may have been Anne's mother that had presented them with some shortbread biscuits contained in the barrel the previous Christmas, On one of their visits to our place Anne brought the barrel with her in which she had placed some home made biscuits, Grantham Gingerbreads I think they were. They went down very well with the family. So when it was our turn to visit them at their place in Stockport I got the idea of baking a couple of sheets of Shortbread, putting them in the barrel and taking it back to Anne and Jim's place. After that it became the thing to do. I can't remember how many round trips the barrel had, but I do recall the Boston Brownies, the Melting Moments, and those lovely Almond Biscuits that Anne always did.

One particular visit will always stay in my mind, for good reason actually. The weather was perfect. One of those cold sunny crisp days of the early new year. I had started learning to drive and we were travelling up the A523 towards a place called Heaviley a mile South of the Stockport City Centre which is where they lived. The children were excited for they always enjoyed seeing their 'Uncle' Jim who was great with kids and they also got on very well with Anne and Jim's child Chris. My two Keith and Millie were at that delightful stage where they are no longer babies and long before the troubles of adolescence. I remember them as being good children, but you tend to forget the bad stuff don't you, as the years go by. I had baked some of my Shropshire Biscuits to put in the tin, that I do recall, but I can't think why I remember that small detail. Everything went well as it always did. Anne had roasted a lovely leg of lamb which we sat down to with all the usual trimmings of mint sauce and roast potatoes. She did not usually make such a fuss, generally serving a few sandwiches was considered enough trouble. Sometimes Jim and Geoff went for a couple of pints at the nearby pub but not on that day. We all sat around talking about old times, while the three children amused themselves without making too much of a racket. It was a lovely visit, but there was something peculiar, something unreal about it.

It was on the following Wednesday evening that we saw it in the newspaper. We already knew about the tragic accident on the M1, it had been mentioned on the Today programme on Radio Four. I always got up early to see Geoff off to work, so we were sitting at the kitchen table, the kids got up later so we always had a nice half hour together every morning. A couple and their child had been involved in a head on collision on the M1 Motorway when a lorry had crossed the central reservation, the lorry driver had passed out due to a stroke. This collision caused a pile up of vehicles, but only the lorry driver and the couple and their child in the front car had died, having said that many drivers and passengers were seriously injured. We both registered it but as no names were mentioned it did not strike us until later. Geoff took the Telegraph which always arrived after he had left for work. But the news was not in the Wednesday edition, but it did appear in the Thursday paper. When he arrived home on Thursday I told him, but waited until Keith and Millie had been put to bed.

'It doesn't make sense. How can it be?' Geoff said.

'But it's there in the paper.'

85

*'They must have got the names wrong,' he said. 'Tell you
what I'll just give Jim a ring, that's the easiest way.' But
the phone rang and rang, nobody was there to answer it.
It was true you see. Jim and Anne, their child Chris had
all been killed in the senseless accident. On the Saturday
the day before we had seen them on the Sunday. It was a
very awkward few days. Geoff was always very hard
headed when it came to spooky things. He had no time for
people who thought they had seen ghosts and to him
fortune telling and even Horoscopes were just a load of
old rubbish. But here was proof of something incredible,
something against all the rules. The science, that was
almost a religion with him, had been proved wrong. Jim,
Anne and their child had entertained us for three hours on
a Sunday afternoon when they had been killed the day
before.*

*We went to the funeral. It was a strange affair. Anne and
Jim were not religious, so who ever had to make the
arrangements thought it would be simpler to have the one
service for all three of them. I have never seen three
coffins in a crematorium before, but it was probably the
best and easiest thing. It was a terrible blow to us, Geoff
missed Jim badly for he was not one for having a lot of
friends. As for me, even though I had only known Anne for
a year or two we were very close.*

*Things went on normally for five years after that before
Geoff came down with heart disease. It had started as
vague pains in the chest which he had put down to
indigestion. The GP sent him up to Stockport for tests and*

he was diagnosed with heart failure. Neither of us thought it was that serious but he only lived another three months. If I had only known it would have been a different three months but we just carried on as normal as if everything was going to be OK. That next Christmas was very hard without him. Keith was fifteen and Millie thirteen by then. I had gone back to work on tele sales, a thankless task if ever there was one, but we needed the money, he died too young for me to qualify for decent widow's benefits. The years went by and suddenly or it seems like suddenly I am on my own living in what seems a big house. Keith had joined the army and was posted abroad. Millie a wandering soul was 'somewhere in England' as they say. She never did anything for long and generally liked every new boy friend better than the one she was with. We kept in touch by the odd postcard and the rare phone call. She thought me very straight laced I'm sure, but I was never convinced that doing exactly what you liked was the way to happiness.

Christmases can get you down, when there is no one to come and no where for you to go. Then every one is supposed to be having a wonderful time, so if you are the odd one out it can hurt. I had been forced to take all the time off between Christmas Eve and the day after New Year. I was stranded at home and feeling very low. I was in the kitchen doing a bit of cleaning when I happened to stray into the pantry and noticed it on the top shelf. It was the biscuit barrel. It gave me a right turn, I can tell you, for I distinctly remember leaving it back at Jim and Anne's place on that last visit. My hands were trembling

*when I reached up and took it down from the top shelf.
Inside it there was a note.*

Hello Alice

**We know how lonely you must be feeling just now, Why
not join us for Christmas Day? We are still at the same
place.**

Anne, Jim and family

*I know it sounds crazy, but there and then I began to bake
some biscuits to put in the barrel. There was not much in
the kitchen cupboards in the way of ingredients so I just
used whatever there was. I did not know whether I would
end up going but felt that I should bake the biscuits
whatever else I did. I ended up with a lovely batch of
'Melting Moments' as, strangely enough, I found all the
necessary ingredients in various cupboards. When they
cooled I put them into the barrel and sat down to watch
the telly. It was the Queen's Speech. Too late to go now.
But I could not rest. Then you can probably guess the rest.
I had a bath. Put my best dress on and did a quick make-
up job using the mirror that stood over the fireplace,
before getting in the car and driving off into a very grey
December early evening.*

*I must tell you that I felt very silly. Done up like a turkey
driving my car on the darkening empty roads. But it all
started to feel very familiar even though it was at least
fifteen years since that last fateful meeting. I arrived at
Heaviley and turned off the Macclesfield Road at the right*

point, it was as if the car knew it s way. Soon I was parking up outside their house and they were out on the pavement to welcome me in. The next few hours passed like a dream. It was never in my mind to question anything. Anne gave me a kiss and took hold of my hand. Jim stood on the other side and we walked into the house which was warm and full of light. Little Christopher ran into my knees and gave them a hug. Strangest of all was Geoff, my Geoff waiting in the lounge for me looking just like I always remembered him. Jim and Anne melted tactfully into the kitchen and me and my lost husband just stood holding hands at a distance looking into each others eyes. 'Alice, I have missed you so much.' was all he said.

Then all was gaiety as we sat around the table in the kitchen and put ourselves around one of the best Christmas Dinners I can ever remember. We drank toasts 'To good times in the past and better times to come.'

Replete with food we retired to the lounge and put a film on the telly I think it was 'It's a wonderful life' with James Stewart. I and Geoff sat together on the sofa while Jim and Anne sat in the two armchairs. It was such an indescribeable pleasure just to hold hands with Geoff again and feel his warm body next to mine.

Honestly I don't remember how I got home. I just recall waking up in bed on Boxing Day morning in a rosy glow of contentment, for now I knew. My life was not all behind me, but the best was yet to be.

After I retired I sold the house in Macc and came back to Stalybridge where I was born. An old aunt on my dad's side had passed away and mentioned me as her only relative. She left me that little place on Lindsay Street. So what with my money from the Macc house and my pension I was suddenly very comfortably off. I could afford to run my little car and go on the odd foreign holiday and if I ever fancied anything I could put my hand in my pocket and buy it.

I know I never used to talk much about my family but I was not being secretive it was just that I was not very lucky that way. By the time I was sixty five I had lost both my children. And that was how I was able to go to two more Christmases with Jim and Alice.

The day I knew that Millie had passed away was another lonely Christmas day. We had not spoken in five years. I had no idea where she was, in later years when ever she did come home there was a scene, we would always fall out about some petty thing or other. The thing was that we had stopped liking each other. I could not do with her idle dirty ways, her continuous secrets, and the snide way she had of talking to me. After the last visit and the last row we spoke on the phone a couple of more times and then silence. She never left me a contact number. I had not seen or heard anything of my son either for a month or two and another lonely day was in prospect. but when I got up that morning I knew. Something felt strange in my chest, other people say they feel it in their water but with me it was a dull ache. I knew my daughter Mildred had gone.

I was very illogical. I don't know what Geoff would have thought. 'Another bee in your bonnet!' "he would have said. Nevertheless I knew where to look. With my heart in my mouth I opened the larder door and there it was on the top shelf as before – The biscuit barrel, inside it was another invitation

Hello Alice

We know how lonely you must be feeling just now, Why not join us for Christmas Day? We are all looking forward to seeing you again

The note was very similar to the last one but not signed. So I went on another ghostly adventure but not until I had baked some more biscuits and got myself ready. First the strange drive along quiet misty roads, then the gloom dispelled by Jim and Anne's warmth. I had a wonderful time seeing Geoff again who just looked the same as last time. He will never age. In addition was little Mildred. Gone was the awkward mixed up creature she became, instead she was a child again, as on that other occasion nearly twenty five years before.

Truth to tell my son Keith was much better at keeping in touch than Mildred, but he always came in company. It was either a barrack mate or some woman he had picked up. They were all pleasant enough but the same person never came more than once. We never got to having a chat about Geoff and the good times of his childhood. He rose to Staff Sergeant signing on for twenty years in the Army. Then the final blow, Keith was killed in Afghanistan in an explosion. This incident took place over the Christmas period, another lonely and miserable time beckoned, but again the biscuit barrel turned up.

On my last visit they were all there. My complete family. Geoff at about thirty three, Mildred at eight years old and finally Keith at the age of ten. Another magical day with no memory of the return journey until I awoke in bed the next morning.

No sign of the biscuit barrel since then. This morning a parcel arrived at the hospital addressed to me. Inside it was the barrel but this time there were biscuits inside and no note. I think that means that they are already here with me even if I cannot see them. When the doctors tell me that everything will be OK I know different. I expect my family to come this afternoon and bring me home with them. I will have just enough time to finish this little story.

So I will say goodbye to you all. Use the money enclosed to buy yourselves something nice, there is £25 for each of you.'

The four women looked at each other when Alice's letter had been read out, then Siobhan spoke first. 'Spooky or what?'

Barbara, the eldest present said, 'Before you ask. I don't want it, the barrel I mean and you can keep the money.' Mary and Beryl joined in both disclaiming the object and money.

'We only have Alice's word for all this. It's quite easy to explain really,' said Beryl, who was always the most sceptical member of the group.

'How do you mean?' asked Mary.

'We're always hearing how wonderful Christmas is supposed to be, and it is when you have young children and a close family, but for many people it has become a nightmare, particularly now when it seems to go on forever.'

'Get to the point, you'll have it raining,' said Barbara who was not enjoying all this talk about death and ghosts.

'As I was saying,' said Beryl, directing a sharp look at Barbara, 'We have poor Alice, all alone, stuck in the house, widowed early in life, and feeling pretty blue. She obviously forgot that she already had the biscuit tin and the rest was just her imagination. I'm not saying that she made it up, mind, she really believed it had happened. But waking up in bed next morning is a bit far fetched. The car cannot have driven itself back from Stockport could it?'

So it was after this unhappy conclusion that Siobhan agreed to keep the Biscuit barrel and cash herself. Mary had the last word. 'Whatever you do, girl, don't put any biscuits in it.'

Alice's biscuit barrel ended up at the bottom of one of her wardrobes in the guest bedroom. She sees it occasionally when she puts a dress away, worn for a special occasion, dresses relegated to this wardrobes are rarely worn again, but she does have a little black two piece number that comes in handy for weddings and funerals. She never mixed up the two, that would be silly. But after the incident of the Barrel she always believed that there was something final about a wedding and something open ended about a funeral.

The Night that Tinkerbelle Died

A memoir of my days in Variety

from the posthumous papers of Jack le Main

I could have done a lot worse you know. . . . . but I always put money away in the good years, and tried not to spend too much when fortune turned against me. I was one of the lucky ones who made it across the gap from Variety onto the telly in the fifties, thus managing to stay the course in show business and continue to make a good living. So now, having reached an age, considerably in advance of discretion, I am staying in what is called a 'Residential Hotel'. Situated in a quiet spot at St Leonards, only five minutes from the prom, the 'Sorrento d'Italia' is a place existing somewhere in the hinterland of human experience that lies between a 'Bed and Breakfast' and a rest home for the elderly.

However, I mustn't complain, for it's a snip at £200 a week all found, but after paying that out there is only enough for the odd pint, the odd punt and the odd 'you know what', but we won't go into that here. Suffice it to say that the staff are very good with the older residents, some of whom would be hard put to manage outside these

95

protective walls.

When Autumn is here, winter is only a month or two
away, and I have always hated the dark nights and
mornings so most days I adhered to a routine that suited
me well. That day I had been out for a quick stroll up and
down the prom in the September sunshine, watching the
last of the holiday makers doing their best, in the best
British way, to have a good time. I had just trotted back
with the Telegraph rolled up under my arm when Mavis,
the manageress, came to my table. 'Mr le Main, I have a
letter for you.' She always addresses everybody as Mr or
Mrs, with the occasional Miss, but as a person of sound
conservative principles, she does not run to Ms. The letter
resided on a silver tray, which is another nice touch they
have here.

An attractive cream laid envelope concealed a hand
written note, done with a fountain pen too. I was most
impressed, and more so, when I saw it was from Maurice
Sylvester. Along with the note in the envelope, was a
cheque made out to me for £50. I perused the contents of
the note my eyes going to the nub of the matter
immediately, for Maurice and I rarely corresponded in
those days.

'You will be distressed to learn that our friend Popsie Black has died. She suffered a massive stroke at home. A blood clot on the brain apparently. She was taken to hospital right away but they could do nothing for her. She was only 67, so young. The funeral service will be at St Paul's in Covent Garden, which I am sure you know as the actor's church. Ten thirty on Thursday next. Have enclosed a cheque to defray your expenses. I'm sure that she would have wanted us both to be there.'

I had known Maurice in better times. Memories of him went back to the Halcyon days after the war. The time when variety was alive and well, when good acts could make good money, before TV got a grip on the nation and people migrated from the back kitchens where they had sat listening to the steam radio around the table playing crib, to the front rooms that then became telly mausoleums , but don't get me started.

After the war I was demobbed at Cleethorpes in December 1945, given a suit of civvy clothes with £7. 10. 0d in its pocket and a recommendation from an officer in my pay book, to the effect that I would make a good clerk or shopworker 'because of my clean habits and neat personal appearance'. To be fair I had worked at the Penn Wholesale Cooperative Society near Wolverhampton up to being conscripted, but the prospect of returning home to slice the bacon and weigh out the tapioca did not appeal. A chap in my platoon Alfie Jordan, who had done a bit of acting, said he could get me on the stage.

'What me on the stage, with two left feet?'I said.

'Give over,' says he, 'You can sing a bit and anyone can act.'

'Act stupid,' says I, but he was right I did get into show business but it was a poor living at first. What's the posh word for it? 'Precarious' that's what it was.

So now we do a slow fade out and put 1953 on the silver screen and I was in a little place not far from Manchester called Ashton under Lyne, in a show at the Theatre Royal, or I would have been but for an unfortunate

circumstance. Over the previous nine months I had been
employed as the Stage Manager with the Delphian
Brilliant All Star Company who put on variety shows.
The company moved between provincial theatres
wherever they could get a booking and generally did a
week or a fortnight at a time.

The role of a stage manager was not one requiring
anything in the way of 'talent', consisting, as it did, in
knocking on the doors of the various 'artistes' to remind
them when they were due to be 'on', accounting for all the
baggage in the way of costumes and props, but most
importantly of all, managing the disposition of props on
the actual stage. However, by the time I first met Maurice
in the toilets of Ashton Indoor Market that opportunity
had withered on the vine. So to put it in actor's parlance, I
was resting.

The reason for this comedown in my fortunes was that the
company manager had done a bunk with our money. He
had disappeared not only with the takings for the current
week but also with the proceeds from the last booking we
had done at the old Manchester Hippodrome. Expecting to
get paid at the end of the week I had been promising my
landlady her money for a fortnight now. She had given me
an ultimatum the night before. She pointed out that her's
was not an organisation supported by Oxfam for the

purpose of the relief of thespians, or was it regulated by
the National Trust, in short it depended upon the financial
contributions of its residents. Unless such a contribution
was received from me by Friday evening I could remain,
otherwise come Saturday morning I would be obliged to
seek fresh accommodation. Not that she was throwing me
out, Mrs Dobbs delicately explained, just putting me in
the picture regarding her financial situation.

Time was hanging heavily that day, as it always does
when one's future is uncertain. Hanging around a small
Northern town, with nothing to do and no money to
spend, cannot be classed as profitable leisure. However,
for the outlay of 4d a very nice cup of hot Bovril could be
purchased in the indoor market which I had been
cautiously sipping in order to waste as much time as
possible, before making my way to the library, where free
newspapers could be studied.

I visited the lavatories in the market before departing
thence, as there were none in the library. It was a
miserable cold day in early October, a steady drizzle was
descending from the sky. I had left my raincoat at the
digs, but did not fancy going back to get it, preferring to
avoid the basilisk stares of the now medusa like Mrs

Dobbs .

I was just discharging the several cups of tea drank with
my breakfast earlier, whilst inspecting one of the
wonderful coats of arms that Thomas Shanks and Co often
embroider upon their urinals, when I caught sight of
something extremely offensive in the form of two men
emerging from one toilet stall. One of these men turned
out to be Maurice Sylvester. A somewhat inauspicious
meeting. The other I recognised as Ned Bryant a young
acrobat with the 'Flying Maldini's' a trio attached to our
company.

Before I could blink, or even do up my fly buttons, a chap
in the next stall had turned and launched himself at the
two queers shouting 'Bloody puffs' as he did so. This
encouraged another couple of fellows, who had been
washing their hands to join him in giving these perverts a
good drubbing. I saw Maurice take a sickening blow to
the side of his head, and young Ned was also the recipient
of a boot towards a delicate part of his lower abdomen.

I had to do something, so I rushed to the door of the

toilets and stood shouting 'Police Police Police!' I am
gifted with a very loud voice so my cries drew
considerable attention. I had done a bit of boxing in the
army, so was reasonably handy with my fists. Going back
in I exchanged a few punches with various fellows, in the
process coming in for a fair amount of punches myself.
Luckily, in the nick of tim,e one of the managers of the
market came into the toilets demanding to know what was
going on. There was a cessation of hostilities at this point,
so Maurice and Stan made tracks, in fact although I have
never witnessed a rat making its way up a drain pipe, I
imagine that those two gave a passable imitation of this
fabulous rodent.

The men left in the toilets, looking sheepish, also sidled
past the manager, whilst I was left behind to explain. 'Bit
of a fight. Other two were getting the worst of it. Thought
I'd better do something?'

'Bloody idiots,' the small but burly market official
commented as he quickly looked around the area. 'No
damage any road!' with that and without saying anything
to me, he stalked off. Looking at myself in one of the
mirrors I saw the bruise on my left cheek that later
developed into a black eye. After delivering a sigh I left
the market hall and after turning down Old Street directed

my steps to the old Library.

I read through the Guardian, the Telegraph (for balance) then had a look at Parismatch and Stern, having little French and less German, it was a case of looking at the pictures with the last two publications. It then took me ten minutes to read both the Express and the Daily Mirror cover to cover, and so finally started on the early editions of the Manchester Evening News and Manchester Chronicle. By five there was no other option but to return to the digs.

No money in my pocket, a cold room, a landlady even more glacial, and no prospects of improvement. Going into the pokey room that only gave a view of a long back alley, too dispirited to even take off my shoes I threw myself onto the bed and began to stare at the ceiling as if the answer to my problems might be found written there. A few minutes later, as my eyelids were beginning to close, came a knock on my door. With a heavy heart I went to open it, expecting to find the irate Mrs Dobbs there, but was surprised to see that it was my neighbour in the next room (Second floor back) none other than Ned Bryant of the earlier 'romantic' encounter.

'I say Le Main, what a stout chap you are. Can I come in

for a second?' I stood aside and he waltzed in sitting immediately on the bed without being invited. I offered him a glass of sherry as one does a fellow thespian, and we made polite noises as to how awful things were, particularly since due to the absconding company manager we were both facing destitution, then he got around to the subject that had prompted his visit.

'Maurice, the chap I was with earlier? He has landlady troubles you know?' Ned had an annoying habit of raising his voice at the end of every sentence which made his every speech resemble a series of questions. 'Mrs Greenhalgh, her name? Sticky old bat if you ask me? Not theatrical you know? Proper landladies are much more understanding of the foibles of two gentlemen?'

Frankly, as the sort of acts he was describing were punishable by imprisonment at the time, I did not comment on the rights or wrongs of Maurice's landlady, but just shook my head in mock sympathy.

'Anyway Maurice wants to meet you? Doing OK he is, variety at the Palace Theatre no less?'

So that was how I met Maurice, at least socially, for the first time when the three of us got together at the 'Theatre and Concert' pub on Oldham Road.

Maurice, who at the time resembled a young Noel Coward, with his slicked back hair, striped suit and correspondent shoes, ordered me a double pink gin without asking what I wanted, Ned had the same and we retired to the snug. Looking around I saw that most of the other customers were men, and oddly assorted couples, young and old in every case. queens, kings, tarts and punters, it was ever thus in those sort of pubs.

Maurice who was always a bit on the outre side took up the running. 'Well! I ask you? I was just in the act of introducing myself to young Ned here, having made ourselves comfy on the bed, you know, trolleys down and all that, when this female imbecile starts belabouring the door, announcing to the world that she knows what we were getting up to and she was not going to have any of it.'

'Fat chance!' snorted Ned, 'I bet she hasn't had any leg-over since Queen Victoria dropped off the twig'

Maurice took up the narrative, ' . . . . and we had just drank the better part of a bottle of Bristol Cream and it doesn't come cheap you know. At first when she started knocking I thought the place was on fire, such a fuss over nothing. When I got up and put on my silk dressing gown on to confront the old kipper she gave me a day's notice to get out, and said she had a good mind to report us to the police and we both had to vacate the place immediately or else!'

I begged him not to go into further details for he was in full spate and the goings on in the market toilets were probably next on the agenda. I was not without sexual experience and had even come across queers before in the ranks but this amount of proximity was still slightly distasteful to me. I hope my disgust did not show on my face, in any case, Maurice went on to tell me everything about himself and his present circumstances which were much brighter than my own and poor Ned's. Maurice was an illusionist, which is another way of saying he had graduated from pulling rabbits out of top hats to making ladies disappear from certain boxes and sawing them in half in other boxes.

Eventually he told me how grateful he and Ned were for my intervention in the Market Toilets, and how he was prepared to to something for me in return. Explaining that he was currently appearing at the Manchester Palace of Varieties in an act he had recently put together. But the problem was that he had just heard of an opportunity in Leamington Spa that would require his presence for a five day period in the next week. He wanted me to take over his act in his absence, and this was how I first got to know Popsie Black who, it turned out was his current lady assistant

Most people remember her as the matronly hotel manager in **Crossing Place**, a part which she played for many years as that dreadful old soap opera creaked on and on. But when I was introduced to Popsie Black she was in her prime. Maurice had arranged for us to meet in the Long Bar on Oxford Street in Manchester on the Sunday morning as they had no performances that day. Popsie was tall, standing at about 5 foot 7 inches. She had striking features, her nose a little too big, her lips were large and sensuous. She could never be described as either plain or pretty. Everyone was always struck by her looks, as they were sometimes by her extravagant deeds – there were never any half measures with Popsie. She was wearing a neat little green suit in a frog spawn pattern with a perky hat that set it off to perfection. I remember that the top of the suit she wore had a way of draping itself behind her that showed off her bottom really well. As for her legs, well! I must not go on, as even at my age the memory of her starts my heart racing.

She said she wanted a Babycham, a drink which Maurice
thought to be extremely naff but she stuck to her guns. I
and he were drinking bottled lager. Settling down in a
corner away from the bar, Maurice made the
introductions.

'But I have no experience, in fact I have never been on
stage before by myself, I mean-' I told them about the
singing and dancing lessons I had been having, and the
times I had done a walk on, in a play but did not mention
my disastrous term in repertory in Leicester, where a
minor Shakespearean role had completely foxed me.
Popsie listened intently to all I had to say. Popsie had that
way that all man eaters have, of making you think you
were the only man in the room worth listening to. She
fixed me with those beautiful light blue eyes of hers as a
snake will hypnotize a rabbit.

The act went like this: Billed as **Dolores del Tito –
Strongest woman in the world**. Me and Popsie came on
immediately after the **Naples Patent Volcano** aka
Giuseppe Frascatelli, late of Ancoats Manchester's Italian
community, who had taken to fire eating as a pleasant
change from selling ice cream. She was dressed in a

knockout costume consisting of about 14 sequins holding
hands, whilst I was resplendent in an evening suit.
Fortunately Maurice was more or less my size. I had a
webbed waistcoat underneath the jacket which was
attached to an invisible wire. This gimmick enabled
Popsie to pick me up and lug me around the stage without
any apparent effort. During this bit of the act Maurice
used to squirm around in her arms and end up in all sorts
of compromising positions which always went down well
with the more knowing members of the audience.

At this point in the act I had to go off and wheel a large
trunk onto the stage containing all manner of weightlifting
gear, and several metal frames to accommodate them,
which I placed on the stage straining my muscles in
simulated agony until the set resembled a medieval torture
chamber. After which six burly male volunteers were
invited up onto the stage to act as 'judges', to ensure that
there was no trickery involved. They were asked to try
and lift various combinations of the weights as arranged
by your truly, which it soon became apparent they could
not or at least only with enormous effort.At this point, in
steps Popsie and easily shifts all the weights into the air
and even begins to juggle with them – interval for
rapturous applause from the women in the audience.

The men were asked to stand aside as Popsie and I did our

unique version of the 'Apache' dance. Which had
similarities to the famous French nightclub version, apart
from the fact that the man was the one getting thrown
around. This was my best bit because, I was rather good at
the Tango, but I did hit the floor quite hard at first until I
got used to falling.

The six just men and true where then ushered back into
centre stage from the wings for the finale of the act, where
a young lady was also asked to come up on stage and
search Popsie to make sure that she was not using any
concealed devices. Popsie then climbed up a ladder onto
an arrangement of three stands, and lay so that one
supported her head, one supported her middle and the
third supported her feet. At this point the percussionist in
the band started a long roll on the kettle drum as I
removed first the stand supporting her feet, and after
walking slowly around her, removed the stand supporting
her head, so that she was balanced on the stand
supporting the middle of her waist in perfect equilibrium.

As the long drum roll continued I came forward with two
silken nooses and asked that the judges examine these
carefully. One of these nooses was then placed over
Popsie's neck to gasps from the audience, (for judicial
 hanging was still a popular sport in those enlightened
times) the other noose was placed around her feet, so that

the two loops were hanging down over the stage from neck and feet. I then, to more gasps from the assembly, casually with a flick of my wrist, tightened the one around her neck, before placing long wooden planks carefully in the loops hanging down to effectively make two swings.

The culmination of the act came when the swings were gradually loaded up first by one man sitting on each swing and then gradually increasing until three men were seated on each long plank and Popsie's body still improbably straight began to act like a see-saw going up and down at each end to the rapturous applause of the audience. At this point the orchestra stopped playing as the grisly spectacle continued, Popsie giving the odd gurgle to provide the impression that this was not a walk in the park.

Then, showing great concern, I rudely pushed the men off the improvised swing, as if things had gone a bit too far, and began to loose the ropes. But Popsie had beaten me to it for with 'one mighty bound' she had freed herself and gracefully jumped down from her perch and was taking a deep curtsey towards the audience.

She then picked me up and tucking me under her arm walked off stage, this last bit always went down very well. I won't go into all the details of the magnets and trickery used in the act for Popsie was no stronger than any other young woman of her age, but I enjoyed my week standing in for Maurice.

*** *** ***

Eleven years later and along came the swinging sixties, both of us were doing well, I on the television and she as a minor pop singer with a few hits to her name. Maurice had gone into TV production and was one of the founders of the Carlton TV Company, they say he made millions. Popsie and I were appearing in the panto **Peter Pan** at the Alhambra Theatre, Bradford. She in the starring role as young Peter and I as the dastardly Captain Hook.

But to go back to the start of my career. Things looked up for me after my stint as a stand in. I obtained another post as a stage manager soon after when Maurice put in a good word for me. By carrying on with my drama and dancing lessons I eventually went back into repertory at the Library Theatre Company in Manchester for four years, and then had another long stint with the Gateway Company in Chester .

One night in a performance of 'Charlie's Aunt' a chap called Hughie Green came to see me after the show. He was already famous for his quiz show called **Double your Money**, but was keen to mount another TV show based on amateur talent that became known as '**Opportunity Knocks**'. He wanted me as a production assistant , both to provide a little coaching for the aspiring amateurs but also to be in charge of the infernal device called the Clapometer that measured the strength of the applause and thus decided which of the acts had won the talent contest.

But if I had done well, Popsie had done better, for she had become one of the singing **Smith Sisters** who did summers at Blackpool and made pop records which led to work on the tellie. A silly argument, prompted by a greedy boyfriend, caused them to break up, but Popsie forged ahead with a solo career as one of the new breed of pop singers in the mould of Dustie Springfield. Her contralto voice and easy folk style was earning her the title of the English Patsy Kline.

 This pantomine booking having come my way because of my fame as the 'Clapometer' man. Every time I strode on as Captain Hook, a rigged up clapometer at the side of the stage would start to move. The panto audience played up to it by clapping wildly every time I appeared. It was great fun and I have never had so much applause for so little effort.

Popsie had recently married. Her husband was the son of a local wealthy textile manufacturer, and younger than she by five years. I saw him hanging around the theatre whilst we rehearsed. He was not an attractive fellow. I did not like his body language nor the smell of it much, for he

carried with him an effluvia that even the most effective
deoderants could not conceal. His complexion was
afflicted by spots and shaving rashes, and his
temperament choleric in the extreme.

Arthur, for that was his name, was much given to rages
and outbursts of violence. My dresser divulged that only
Arthur's father's money had kept his son out of prison on
more than one occasion. Arthur suffered insanely from
jealousy. He did not like to have Popsie out of his sight
for long. He even went to the ridiculous lengths of
booking a seat for each and every performance of the
show.

I had always carried a bit of a torch for Popsie going back
to those five weeks in 1953 when I did my stand in for
Maurice in the weight lifting act. Popsie, to be fair, never
gave me any encouragement, but that did not stop us
being good chums. Over the years we had kept in touch,
and even met up on occasions whenever we happened to
be in the same locality.

I was fascinated by this business of her terrible husband,
and like all 'old women' of the masculine gender was
anxious to have a good chat with someone in the know.
One Sunday evening a week after the first night I found
myself in the Alexandra, a Bradford pub patronised by the
'haunters of woodlands and glades' and their fellow
'cottagers' where I bumped into my dresser, Clive, a
dapper little chap with a springy step and a shock of
blonde hair that stood up as if in permanent alarm. He

knew a great deal more about Popsie's affairs than I did, details he was happy to pass on to me.

The lady in question was becoming a little tired of occupying a gilded cage and longed to spread her wings. Arthur, her oppressive husband, always waited backstage after every performance. The night before, being a Saturday, my dresser had witnessed a set to between them. The couple had put on a spectacular shouting match, which could be heard all over the house.

'So she turned around to him and said "You can bugger off" yes that is exactly what she said. "You can take all your money, your big house and stuff them up your arse" those were her very words, just as I'm sitting here.

At this point, Clive took a long drink out of the Gin and It I had purchased for him before continuing with the narrative. 'Then I happened to notice that she had some luggage with her that a taxi driver was carrying into her dressing room, so she must have moved out that day.' He then went on to say that Popsie had her eye on the assistant stage manager in the show. 'Isn't it funny how jealousy always seems to cause the very thing that it seeks to avoid?' he asked, moving a little too close to me for comfort.

After learning this I made it my business to keep an eye on Popsie, and whenever I saw her awful husband giving her a hard time back stage, I used to saunter over and stand staring at him, until he got the idea and left her alone. My looks have never inspired fear but I do have a certain presence, it's been said.

'It's terrible Jack,' she confessed to me one night in the wings whilst waiting to go on together, 'He's hired these two thugs, and they follow me about outside. I can't go anywhere without seeing them.'

'Those two big coloured lads? I think I've seen them.'

'Yes they wait outside the theatre in a car.'

'Why don't you complain to the police?'

'Hardly seems worth it, there are only two weeks of the show left. I've got a recording contract in the states and chance of a few shows. You won't see my heels for dust.'

And so we come to the night, the night that Tinkerbelle died. We had got about two thirds through the show. The house was packed, another Saturday night I recall. It was a brilliant set all done in green in the foreground with a blue ocean and sky at the back. A pirate ship with the Jolly Roger could be seen floating in the distant bay.

I was attired in my role as the dastardly Captain Hook, and she was done up splendidly as Peter Pan in a purple jerkin and green tights, an outfit that did wonders for her gorgeous legs.

We were tangling in a duel, cutlass to cutlass. Sparks were flying from the metalwork. Old Popsie had a glint in her eye and was laying on with the ferocity of Mc Duff, this was done to the accompaniment of the 'Ride of Valkyries' by the orchestra. At one point in the affray she winked and beckoned with an arch of the eyebrow. Obediently I went into the clinch and we locked swords.

'Can you do me a favour?' She whispered with her mouth close to my ear. I said Yes, and she told me what she wanted me to do. It was a tall order, but to a Sir Galahad like me, what is the odd perilous quest but just another thing in a day's work.

The sword play came to an end when the band struck up with the '**Never smile at a crocodile**' song and Popsie and I ran off stage when the big rubber effigy of this beast was dragged on by a couple of ropes. Tiger Lily and Wendy then did their duet to the music with audience participation by clapping in time to the music.

This number always went down a storm, because it gave the scantily clad two young beauties lots of opportunities to swagger up and down the stage displaying their natural assets to the great interest and delight of all the grandads, uncles and dads in the audience.

The little fairy Tinkerbelle was deeply in love with Peter Pan, so the intrusion of Wendy and the consequent alienation of his affections had broken her heart. Tiger Lily and Wendy were extremely concerned about Tinkerbelle because her light was on the wane, and growing very dim.

Now between ourselves, and please don't tell the children, the role of Tinkerbelle was played by a 5 Watt light bulb on the end of a wire, with a device in the circuit to turn the brightness up and down. The bulb was pinned to the costume of one of the lost boys who lurked in the dim

118

light at the back of the stage.

'Oh look children' said Tiger Lily, 'Tink's light is growing dim. She is going to die.'

'What shall we do to save poor little Tinkerbelle?' cried Wendy (a statuesque blonde bursting out of her Austrian dirndl)

'Let's see if the boys and girls in the audience can help,' suggested Tiger Lily (a very striking olive skinned brunette dressed in buckskins).

Wendy had an idea, 'Let's all say together that "We believe in fairies"'

'Boys and Girls,' says the lovely Tiger Lily, 'Let's all say it together, "I believe in fairies.", "I believe in fairies,"'

Then unexpectedly the tiny light, suddenly went out.

Backstage there were ructions taking place, for Popsie, whose unprofessional plan it had been to sneak out of the theatre during the performance, had been prevented from leaving by her husband's two thugs.

She had changed into her ordinary apparel and had decided to abscond with her boyfriend by going out through the auditorium. They had made their way to the wings carrying a couple of suitcases, but unfortunately, before they could descend to the level of the stalls by the side stairs, one of the heavies spotted them and a scuffle broke out.

In the ensuing rough house somebody's foot caught in the wire, Tinkerbelle's wire, and broke it, or damaged the circuit, in any case that was the reason why the light was extinguished.

Back on stage they were improvising, both aware that the light had gone out.

'Boys and Girls, you are not trying hard enough. Little

Tink can't hear you, which is why her light has gone out, no I mean, grown so dim,' said Wendy.

'Let's all say it together again,' cried Tiger Lily, inwardly vowing that this was going to be her last pantomime season.

'I BELIEVE IN FAIRIES,
'I BELIEVE IN FAIRIES,
'I BELIEVE IN FAIRIES,
'I BELIEVE IN FAIRIES,
'I BELIEVE IN FAIRIES,
'I BELIEVE IN FAIRIES,
'I BELIEVE IN FAIRIES,
'I BELIEVE IN FAIRIES.

As this did not have the effect of miraculously healing the wire, the mums and dads, grandma's and granddads, and even the aunts and uncles were asked to join in:-

'I BELIEVE IN FAIRIES,

'I BELIEVE IN FAIRIES,
'I BELIEVE IN FAIRIES,
'I BELIEVE IN FAIRIES,
'I BELIEVE IN FAIRIES,
'I BELIEVE IN FAIRIES,
'I BELIEVE IN FAIRIES,
'I BELIEVE IN FAIRIES.

The light remained stubbornly out.

'Oh Wendy! What shall we do now?' cried the beautiful brunette.

'I know,' said Wendy ' We shall go into the woods and find the fairy doctor to come and cure little Tink. But, Oh look! I can see the crocodile swimming close by, in the river.' (here she gestured to the conductor of the orchestra) 'Why don't we all sing the crocodile song again?'

 Wendy left the stage, followed by all but one of the lost boys. The band cranked up and for the next five minutes Tiger Lily (and the remaining lost boy) pranced up and down the stage leading the audience in a spirited rendition of

'Never Smile at a Crocodile,'

In the wings Brenda Shuttleworth aka Glenda Delight aka Wendy was drawing heavily on a Woodbine cigarette and cursing like a docker,'Where the f*** is that c*** of an assistant stage manager, what's his name? Eric? Isn't he supposed to fix stuff that breaks down?'

The man standing in the wings next to her, responsible for cues and general stage management during the show was equally distraught. Nothing like this had ever happened in twenty years in Show Business. He was standing with the bulb control box in his hands. His language betrayed his frustrated nature.

'Don't ask me. I haven't seen the little bastard for ten minutes . Anyway some bleeder has cut the f******* wire. That's why the bleeding little t*** of a bulb won't work.'

'Why don't you get another bulb and some wire. It can't be that hard. I'll go back on, and do another number if necessary. We can't let Tinkerbelle die. Tinkerbelle must never die!' said Brenda/Glenda stubbing out her cigarette with her foot on the stage.

The stage manager rounded on her savagely. 'I'm not f******* daft you know, even though I might look it.' he hissed. 'There's a big barney going on in the corridor. Five blokes knocking all colours of s*** out of each other. If you fancy trying to get to the stores past them, be my guest!'

Glenda gave a shrug, dived down into the pit first to brief the conductor, and then returned to the stage to go down with the ship if necessary. The absence of both Peter Pan and Captain Hook from the show and the untimely death of Tinkerbelle meant that a great deal of the remainder had to be made up on the spot.

Four times through '**Gilly Gilly Ossenfeffer Katzenellen Bogen by the Sea'** will tax even the most heroic of constitutions and they even did "Partridge on a pear tree " and a selection of Christmas Carols. As an ingenious plot variation one of the lost boys pretended to be a villain, after vengeance on the person of Wendy, by donning Captain Hook's three cornered hat and grasping a wooden sword, he lurked on the stage at the back, behind some stand up props, menacingly.

'Where is the naughty man,' Wendy cried.

'He's behind you!' shrieked the infants,

Wendy turns and see no man, 'Where is he? I can't see him.' Man had disappeared behind props, she turns back to the audience, 'Where is he? I can't see him.'

'He's behind you!' shriek the infants again, and so on ad nauseam.

The show lasted thirty minutes longer than normal and was said by many to be the best production of Peter Pan they had ever seen.

The unseemly affray referred to by the unfortunate deputy stage manager was fought between myself, Eric the errant stage manager, soon to become one of Popsie's men, on one side, and the grieving husband and his two thugs on the other. Popsie hovered on the edges of the scrap and kicked the odd unfriendly shin when she got the chance. Eventually some more men from the company joined in and the three villains were seen off. Popsie and Eric finally got into their long delayed taxi and were off.

Although I never saw her again in the flesh she used to send me a Christmas card every year. We had the odd phone conversation, but our paths never crossed professionally. We were always promising to get together but we never did. Her new romance did not last very long. I think she was a bit too intense and tended to burn her men out quickly.

I was all right apart from the broken collarbone and the two black eyes I sustained in the rough house. I managed the remaining two weeks of the season by wearing a sling, the black eyes looked to be in character. Wendy aka Glenda was promoted to Peter Pan, and Tiger Lily became a rather sallow Wendy. My dresser did a very good Tiger Lily in drag.

The funeral was very well attended for there is something special about that church (St Paul's Covent Garden) and you should visit if you ever get the chance. I saw Maurice and we shared a few yarns about the old times and had a few drinks remembering Popsie.

As for Tinkerbelle she made full recovery in the very next performance and by all accounts is still in vibrant health. She will be appearing in a theatre near you soon. I am sure that she would love to see you there.

The Dragon of Wu Pi

Being a story for children of all ages

Many years ago, before even the house where you live
was built, even before your Grandad and Grandma were
born, and further back than even before the town where
you live was put together, there lived a dragon in a cave
on the side of a mountain. The mountain was called
Mount Upto. This mountain was in a big country called
China. China is far away to the East. It would take Daddy
a long time to drive there, even if his car could cross seas
and oceans, and it is such a long distance away that a jet
plane takes ages to fly all the way there.

Now a dragon is not something that you can go and look
at in the zoo, and you won't see one in any television
programs either, because there are not very many dragons
about these days, and the ones that do exist tend to be shy
and keep out of the way. I had better tell you what this
particular dragon that lived in China looked like, then if
you do happen to spot a dragon you will know what it is.
This dragon was very large, nearly as big as one of those
lorries that go swishing past Daddy's car on the motorway
leaving lots of spray behind them. I say that it was as large
as a lorry but it was not quite as noisy, but if you do ever
see one on a motorway I would tell Daddy to put his foot
down on the accelerator, for dragons can be quite nasty
creatures. It is a pity that they are so dangerous because
they are very pretty to look at, being coloured a lovely

green, with bits of red, orange and silver here and there. Dragons can breathe out fire. Have you ever noticed how your breath looks like smoke on a cold and frosty day? Well, dragons can pour fire from their mouths just like you can make smoke on chilly days, not only this but they can fly through the air too because they have large leathery wings. But the very worst thing about them is that they like to eat people, after they have cooked them with their fiery breath.

Dragons could do magic things, for instance they could turn themselves into the likeness of anything else in a second. Say a dragon wanted to look like an elephant, well all the dragon had to do was say to itself 'I will be an elephant' and POOOF, just like that it would be an elephant. They could also turn themselves into people when they liked. So be careful for there might be a dragon lurking in your class at school looking like a teacher and you would not know from looking at them. Dragons were nasty creatures most of the time, and therefore, as I said before, it was best to avoid them, but now and then they would do a good thing, just to be awkward I suppose?

There is a Chinese story of a dragon who turned himself into a poor old man. One day when this dragon was flying over the town, the dragon looked down and saw an old poor man being beaten by his cruel son. The son was too lazy to work and relied on his father to ask for money for him so they could buy food and drink for themselves. The son used to lie on the sofa at home all day doing nothing, while his poor aged father went out into the streets of the town to ask people to give him money. If the old man did not come back with a lot of money his son used to beat him with a big stick. The wicked young man made his father's life very unhappy. The dragon found out about all this by turning itself into a bird and perching near the windows of the house where the old man and his son lived.

His father returned early on a certain day. The son counted the money, which was not enough, so he took down his stick to begin beating the poor old man. But the son made a big mistake, for this was not his father. It was the dragon who had used magic to make himself into the image of the old man. One second his father was trembling before him the next second a mighty dragon was standing over the evil son. When the real father returned from his begging much later he could find no trace of his naughty son. Instead, near the couch, where his son used to lie, he found a heap of smoking ashes but among the ashes were ten bright diamonds.

The old father never found out that the dragon had eaten his son, but he took the jewels to a shop and sold them for a huge amount of money, so he never again had to go about the streets asking other people for money for he had enough to live on for the rest of his life. He put the ashes into a bowl and placed it on top of the table. He did not know that the ashes in the bowl were not those of his son, just the ashes of the stick that his son once used to beat him with.

At one time thousands of years ago there were many dragons in China. There were also witches and wizards who did bad magic to hurt people with, but there were also priests who did good magic to fight the bad stuff of the witches and wizards, not to mention the bad magic of the dragons as well. Ancient China was a strange and weird place where almost anything could happen, sometimes there was too much rain and the crops drowned in the fields, sometimes too much sun and the grain withered and died, and even when the weather was good there was always the fear of earthquakes and volcanoes. And in the odd chance that all was well with the weather and everything else, there were robbers and warring armies wandering around the place causing misery. No, Ancient China was not a good place to live and if I were you I would stay living where you are with mummy and daddy and be grateful that you were not born in the China of old.

Now this story is about dragons and one dragon in particular. This dragon was called Tang. Like most dragons Tang did many wicked things. The story has a brave boy in it and two girls, one that was nice and one that was not so nice. Also there are lots of other people in it like your mummy and daddy and your uncles and aunts, but there are also some very wicked and nasty persons, but you will meet them all in the pages that follow. The setting of the story, where it happened, was in a village called Wu Pi which is pronounced 'Wooo Peee' just so you know how it sounds. The houses of this village had been built on the sides of a steep mountain. In front of the mountain there stood a large flat area that was called the Plain of Shang. Across that plain quite a few miles away stood a large town called Shanglo. It took nearly a day to reach the town of Shanglo by crossing the plain of Shang. As there were no cars or trucks in Ancient China you had to use a horse or donkey, and a cart if you had anything to carry. It was very slow travelling in a cart but quicker than walking.

The people in the village of Wu Pi grew plants and trees and kept animals so they had plenty of rice, bread, meat, vegetables, and fruit to eat. The food that they did not eat they used to sell in the town and use the money they got to buy other things that they could not make themselves or grow. They grew the rice on terraces like narrow strips of earth on the sides of the mountain, and used the fields below to graze their animals and grow other crops with fruit trees here and there.

A person living in the town of Shanglo who wanted to journey to the village of Wu Pi had to cross the wide and flat Plain of Shang. It was a most dreary and bleak place for there always seemed to be a cold wind blowing and there were no trees to provide shelter from the bite of the bitter wind.

The Village of Wu Pi

Once a traveller had crossed the plain there was still the mountain to climb for the village stood half way up the slope of Mount Up To, which was so high that the top was always in the clouds. To reach the village you had to follow a narrow path which went first to the left and then back to right, as mountain paths always do, as it wound its way up the steep slope. By the time the weary traveller reached some of the way to the village they would have to pause to get their breath back and rest their animals for their horses would also be tired out. Eventually the path began to level off and then finally to go down slightly, but as the path went downwards it became narrower. So narrow that it became difficult for donkeys loaded with goods to get through. The very worst thing was that this narrow path led past the mouth of a cave in the rocks situated at the side of a steep cliff. In this cave lived the wicked dragon Tang.

Crossing the mouth of Tang's cave was a very dangerous business. Tang was a dragon who had good moods and bad moods. In the right mood he could be very kind but it was not a good idea to be anywhere near him when he was in a bad temper. Some days he would eat any traveller that happened to pass the mouth of his cave, while at other times he would let everyone go on their way without troubling them at all. Sometimes when he had eaten someone who disagreed with his tummy he would let out a random stream of flame and it was very bad luck for anyone passing the cave when this happened for they would be burned up.

Now I don't suppose that you have ever been eaten by a dragon, because if you had been you would not be reading this, would you? But I can tell you that it is a very nasty thing being eaten by a dragon and not something I would recommend to anyone, even someone I did not like. Just like you and I dragons prefer to have their food cooked. Imagine what you would say if your mummy gave you a slice of frozen Pizza and a frozen fish finger straight from the freezer, broke two raw eggs over it and said 'There you are Beatrice, now eat it all up.' It would not be nice would it? Well, dragons feel the same way about their food. Before they eat anything they like it to be cooked just right. The trouble is that a dragon's favourite food is little boys and girls, particularly little girls!

A dragon has a big fire in his tummy so he can breathe out fire anytime he wants to, which makes cooking very easy for him. But he has to be very careful not to breathe out too much fire or he will overcook or burn his food and nobody likes to eat burnt food, which is why mummy always scrapes the black bits off the toast into the kitchen sink when she burns the bread slices in the toaster.

Having the dragon Tang living in a cave so near could have been a problem for the villagers, but the dragon never ate any of the people from the village who could pass to and fro in front of his cave without worrying about him. You see the dragon knew all the people in the village very well because he had made something called an agreement with them. In case you do not know what an agreement is I will tell you. An agreement stands between two or more people when they have promised that they will either do something or not do something, and as long as they both abide by this promise the agreement remains in force.

The dragon Tang had an agreement with the villagers that he would not eat any of them, but in return they had to provide one of their girls for him every year. This was a very bad thing from the point of view of most of the people in the village, particularly the girls and their parents, but some of the others thought it was a price worth paying, because the dragon protected the village from robbers and bandits, and other kinds of naughty people who wanted to steal from them or even kill them for no reason. As I have said, nobody could get into the village unless they went past the dragon's cave. And we all know what happened to people from other places when Tang was at home.

Life in those ancient times in China was very hard, particularly for poor people like the ones that lived in the village of Wu Pi. But because they had the dragon, nobody could push the villagers of Wu Pi around. In China at the time there were constant wars going on between rebel armies and warlords. These large groups of men did not carry their own food around with them but just robbed and took what they wanted from the local people wherever they pitched camp on the way to their next battle. Very often the poor farmers went hungry because all the food they had grown was taken away from them by these parasites. The protection of the village by Tang meant that the villagers of Wu Pi always had plenty to eat, unlike other villages who were at the mercy of the armies.

A war lord called Pong tried to rob the village of food once. He marched some of his men up the mountain path to the village to demand bread and rice for his army. Luckily for them Tang was not at home that day, but later, when Tang returned, Pong had reason to regret his actions, for looking down the mountain to the plain, where most of his army waited in their tents, he saw the dragon descend upon them from the sky. Suddenly every tent was on fire and as the men streamed out they were burnt up by Tang's fiery breath. Tang also picked out a few of Pong's men for food and took them back to his cave one by one in his mighty jaws. As Pong tried to return down the path he was snatched himself and the men with him were then burned up as they tried to run past the cave.

But the villagers all knew there was a terrible price to pay for this peace that they enjoyed and it was a very high price. Every year on a given day at a given time a girl had to go to the cave of the dragon. This girl never came back

The Scrooge Syndrome

Being a short synopsis of the best selling novel which I have not yet written.

Charlie Elliot lay bleeding and still in a stifling boggy hollow. Such light as there was filtered down through layers of dark green; and here, at the very bottom layer, only the very odd glimmer of the sky could be seen through the dense canopy of leaves that stretched above him. The cries of many birds and small mammals filled the void with sound and the odd drop of condensation fell on his face from the impossibly verdant foliage above him. He had been drifting in and out of consciousness for some time now. One part of his brain knew that something was very wrong, but the main part of his mind was reluctant to accept the full extent of his situation. He was at least comfortable, nothing was hurting too much, although he was aware that a creature was nibbling at the small toe on his left foot. When he eventually tried to move, the only part of his body that responded was his left leg and arm, then only by a fraction of an inch. The rest of his body lay immobile as if it weighed twenty tons.

Why, he asked himself, was he, an extremely successful and wealthy man, lying here, hundreds of miles from any form of civilisation in the South American jungle?

Memory was slow in returning. He recalled that there had been three days of brutality. Forced to march with a heavy burden and beaten every time he stumbled, through mile after mile of the thickest and most overgrown of tropical rain forests. Then after arriving in this hollow, his captors had taken turns to beat him. But because he had landed in an awkward place, where there were low branches and bushes, many of the blows were deflected or not delivered with full force, none of the men having the initiative to move their prisoner to a more open spot in order to finish him off more efficiently.

As full awareness returned it came to him that he had a great thirst, that his body was covered in small wounds and finally, when he tried to call out, that he could not speak. He practised making popping sounds, and raspberries with his lips, tutting sounds with tongue and palate, but even these primitive means of communication seemed to have deserted him.

Nature took pity on Charlie as he drifted into another long slumber, but when he awoke again it was in pitch darkness, a blackness so oppressive and vast that it was almost possible to touch it, so for another hour, until sleep mercifully returned, he was condemned to lie there and take stock and recall the precise circumstances of his fall.

When he awoke for the third time it was again day, judging by the slivers of light he could see above him. But then, most terrible of all, came the overwhelming sensation that his death was very near. Now a great weakness and a colossal lassitude assailed him. He faced the certainty that in his current situation, without help, he would last only a few more hours. By noon of the second day, at last, with the return of his full mental capacities, the full realisation as to the means, whys, and wherefores, the disastrous misjudgements that had put him into this situation, finally dawned on him. This drove the last shred of hope out of him like a sledge hammer hitting an egg.

Elliot found that he could move the left side of his mouth up to produce a lopsided smile. His story, though ultimately tragic, was not without a certain irony, for it was the very penny pinching creed, he had extolled, that led to his undoing. It was this realisation that brought the rueful half smile to his face. Smiling encouraged him so Charlie decided to try and move his arm again. The limb

slid about five inches away from his body, but, try as he
might, he could not lift it off the ground. His left arm was
now resting near a small broken branch. Exerting a great
effort he tried to grip this branch. As he did so he heard a
loud scream from nearby. What he was gripping was not a
branch but the tail of a creature, the nature of which he
could not even guess at. Using all his remaining strength
he squeezed again and was rewarded when the trapped
animal gave another scream. Altogether he managed ten
squeaks before the creature escaped when his grip
weakened too much.

Again he slept, but when he awoke discovered that he was
no longer alone. Three small brown skinned naked Beatle
hairdos were standing over him. Having heard of the
atrocities commited by some of these tribes Elliot braced
himself for the inevitable slow torture that would surely
follow, but to his surprise these men were quite solicitous
of his welfare. First by letting him drink a small judicious
amount of tepid water from a skin they carried, then by
constructing a stretcher from skilfully cut branches and
leaves and installing him tenderly upon it. It hurt when
they moved him from the jungle floor. The pain made him
pass out. When he opened his eyes the next time he found
himself lying on an approximation of a proper bed, in a
small hut composed like the stretcher, of leaves and
branches. As far as he was able to tell, he had been
washed and his wounds attended to in a primitive but
highly efficient manner. His body was arrayed in a long
white nightgown and he lay on his back on the bed.

*** *** ***

The inexplicable disappearance of Charlie Elliot was thought to be highly unsatisfactory from several points of view. His publishers, who had reaped golden rewards from his first book, were demanding a sequel. His family and literary agents, wanted the golden goose to keep producing more eggs in the way of their share of the royalties. Finally, his audience, the general public, including those who had not even read his book, wanted their curiousity about the mystery of him dropping out of the known world to be satisfied.

Elliot was famous for being a well read author, although he had only written one book. This slim volume entitled

'Dynamic Pessimism -or Why You are Right to look after yourself and to distrust Do Gooders'

had made not only his fortune but millions for everybody associated with its publication. Having gone through 15 editions, sold 20 million copies and having been translated into 30 languages, it was truly a literary phenomena. But if he had found unlikely fame in the role of an author , Elliot had in his time played more than a few other roles, amongst which were: Petty thief (mainly supermarkets, never graduating to burglary), Journalist (Adverts, Births, Weddings, and deaths mainly), General Dealer (car thefts and fraud), Husband of four women, (the last marriage bigamous), Family man (children numbered nine, six in wedlock). The children, at least the ones he acknowledged, and his wifes uniformly hated him, but were happy to take his money.

His book (to summarise it in a nutshell) stated baldly that everything universally acknowledged to be good, was really bad, and contrariwise, all that was regarded as evil and to be discouraged, was actully good and salutary in every way. He had hit upon, with unconcious serendipity, a way of summing up the dark thoughts of even the most charitably inclined amongst us, and the doubts that exist in the minds of the silent majority regarding the veracity of the views put forward by the modern neo-liberal consensus.

According to Charlie, **Charity**, if such a thing has to exist, should suffer from agoraphobia. It begins and ends at home and never should venture abroad. One's primary responsibility was to oneself first and if there was anything left over from self care, it should be devoted first to family and then to friends in that order. The concept of devoting any care, money or effort in any other spheres than these was idiotic and would inevitably cause more problems than it could ever remedy. If every person in the world cared to follow this admirable creed most of their problems would be solved.

He stated that the gaining and keeping of money, was the most important thing in our lives. only the dead need not worry about their finances.

The kindness of strangers was described as a miracle, and

extremely difficult to explain, for Elliot found it impossible that anyone should do anything for nothing. On the whole he explained, that thieves and liars were to be preferred to enlightened liberals, for at least ne'er do wells could be trusted to deceive, whereas the do-gooders were totally unreliable because they believed their own lies and would try to foist them off an anybody foolish enough to listen, who would in turn go on to promulgate these false misery causing creeds.

His book rounded up all the Holy Cows of the liberal theology, he penned them into an Abbatoir and after saguinary slaughter turned them into meat pies for the masses.

What has been the result of all the charitable aid lavished by organisations such as Oxfam in obscure foreign fly infested places? Are they any better off now? Would they ever be any better off?

Where do all the 'homeless' Big Issue' sellers live? If they are truly homeless why do they not have the decency to freeze to death in cold winters?

Why do we need to 'Save the Children'? Is not looking after our own children sufficient? Who decides which children will be saved, and from whom or what are they to be saved?

He pointed out the folly of dope smoking simplistic pop singers organising concerts with the aim of abolishing hunger. Not only was this ridiculous in itself, but the funds raised were an insult to those in places of famine who were using more constructive ways of solving these problems. In most of these cases the money raised tended to get into the wrong hands, buying guns instead of butter.

Elliot also opined that Goverment Welfare policies encouraged idleness producing and fostering a large ever growing underclass of claimants. He proposed that all welfare benefits, including pensions should be rigorously means tested and only paid in cases of proven destitution. Workhouses should take care of many claimants, these to be run at a profit if possible.

Political correctness was deemed suppression of speech, which he said originated in the many useless universities springing up in recent times teaching futile subjects. He proposed the abolition of the student loan agency and the re-institution of maintenance grants and free tuition for the top 5% of A level students. Students not qualifying in this way could still attend universities but would pay commercial rates of interest on their loans.

He reminded his readers that 'Goodwill' only stretched to men of goodwill. All priests and religious ministers were parasites, and religious people their dupes.

An income tax rate of 4p in the £ was quite sufficient to run the army for the defence of the realm. All other services would be funded privately or through charities, including the sickness service as he called it, for in his

144

view the 'NHS'had nothing to do with health, only sickness.

Although the market for 'self improving' books was normally limited, one astute literary agent thought that in the then current uncertain times, the book could prove to be a success. After publication of the book Charlie's ideas found many who were sympathetic. A typical attitude being 'Not that I agree with everything he says, but I do feel that there is some good sense in the book.' The pseudo enlightened tone of the work made it 'sort of' OK to be hard hearted to such an extent that in the years following many charities found that their fund raising efforts thwarted by a new cynicism rife amongst subscribers.

The difficulties faced by the charities were in direct contrast to the blessed state of the author who soon found himself to a be new resident in Lichtenstein, where he was regularly in receipt of the huge royalty cheques that his ingenious work generated. These after skilful laundering through huge 'losses' in local consenting casinos were invested in Swiss numbered accounts. It must be said that success had little effect of the character of Charlie Elliot, who continued to live the life of a serial confidence man, moving around from place to place, rarely paying hotel bills and even sneaking out of restaurants without settling the bill. This strategy was useful in both avoiding paying local taxes and also acted to stymie the demands of his family and relatives for money.

When his publishers suggested a 'Round the World' book signing tour, he fell in with it gladly. He would probably have survived the experience if his greed had not led him astray. It was a sad chapter of disasters that condemned him, but some would say that it was all due to a breach in the dam of accumulated bad Karma that swept down the slope and swept him away to infinitiy.

You may ask how I came to know all this? The answer to your question is that I had the honour to be Charlie's agent. For ten years or more I negotiated deals for new editions, screwed ever larger royalty payments out of the publishers, and to this day I now act for his estate, and will do until either I drop from the twig or the book goes out of copyright. I do have three sons at Eton and three ex-wives by the way, but I digress.

I remember my last phone conversation with him, reversed charges from Cancun in Mexico. 'You can only sign so many books, Maurie,' he told me. 'There's a limit to the number of faces you can smile up at, and the common place things that you have to say to them, start to leave your mouth like impacted back molars. Even when the publisher tells you that each stint is worth £10K in sales, you start to long to be left alone, and you end up hating the punters.'

That phone call took place in 2015 whilst he was travelling through Central America on the whistle stop book signing jamboree. I was never to speak to him again. The story, when it finally surfaced went like this.

At the end of a long and very annoying queue in a large but stuffy bookshop in beautiful downtown Cancun close to the Kukulan Plaza, there came to his table a distinguished looking man who declined the signed copy offered by the author. Every inch the Spanish Grandee the gentleman sported a waisted vicuna suit, under which he wore a black velvet waistcoat. His shirt white and immaculate completed by a black tie. On his feet highly polished English shoes by John Church.

Charlie's neck was tired from gazing up from the table at his subscribers, so it was the shoes of the gentleman that had first caught his attention. He knew that particular pair of unobtrusive black Oxfords to be priced at a cool £350. He therefore looked up into the face of this man who waited impassively before the table. The grandee merely smiled and handed over an envelope to the author. The man waited silently until Charlie opened the envelope and saw that it contained a gilt edged invitation card . To his amazement he also saw that there was money in the envelope.

'Slightly more than you earn as an after dinner speaker I assume?'

Charlie looked at the many likenesses of Benjamin Franklin that stared back at him from inside the envelope and asked, 'How many will be there. I'm tired just now. You may have to get someone else for an afterdinner speech.'

'Why senor?' began the man, raising his dark eyebrows just a fraction, 'there will only be you and I, a discreet servant or two to look after us and maybe pour the wine, perhaps a couple of women, if they please you? If you like and prefer it we can dine completely alone?'

'But why? This is a lot of money, Mr . . . ?'

'My name is Garcia, Esteban, you may have heard of me? . . . But no matter, I am a rich man Senor Elliot I can well afford to pay for those things that please me. I have wanted to meet you for I admire the sentiments in your excellent book.'

The address given was a short cab ride from the hotel, that and the saving of the cost of his dinner, prompted Elliot to accept the offer.. After a long and extremely good meal, during which the conversation had been fairly sparse, they retired to a comfortable area on a patio with a glorious view for Senor Garcia's villa stood on a high promontory from where it was possible to look down both upon the town, the beach, but also far out into the glittering sea. The grandee asked his guest a few questions the answers to which seemingly satisfied him.

'I believe that you have an interest in the Mayan civilisation?' Senor Garcia suddenly said. How the grandee could have known about Charlie's all consuming passion was a mystery, but the statement was certainly true.

This interest in the obscure South American ancient culture was atypical of the man whose principal pre-occupations were money and his own comfort, in that order, and to the exclusion of anything else, as I knew to my cost. In all the time I knew him he had never paid for a meal with me, a drink, or even a taxi ride. Five years before his meeting with the grandee, Charlie found himself confined to bed in a seedy hotel just outside Marseilles. He had been invited to a literary dinner where he had been plied with food and too much red wine in the form of a very superior Beaune. With two bottles of this wonderful stuff inside him he had not felt the pain of his tumble down some stone steps outside the restaurant. But with sobriety came the pain, whereupon it was discovered he had broken his ankle.

Too tight fisted to have himself properly looked after he spent the next three weeks in the sordid little hotel. Confined to his room and relying on rather surly staff to fetch and carry for him. The only book in the place written in English was an encyclopeadic, profusely illustrated account of the Mayan Civilisation and its relics. As the long weeks drifted by this book became a source of great fascination to him. Back on his feet again he soon followed up on his new interest and had attended the odd auction where such relics could be bargained for. So by the time of his meeting with Senor Garcia, he was by way of being a considerable collector.

'If you can spare me a minute or two I will show you my

poor little selection,' said Garcia with commendable humility for when Charlie saw what the Senor had to display he was nearly blown out of the water, for there, adjacent to the patio was a room in which stood a couple of glass cases containing the most perfect Mayan pottery, carved jade and glasswork that Elliot had ever seen, better even than the pictures in his books on the subject.

To Charlie's surprise his host was quite forthcoming about the origins of his treasures. There was a ruined city of the Mayans deep in the jungle less than a hundred miles away from where they stood he said. The place could be reached best by plane and then boat as a river ran nearby, or rather between the river and the site it was only a matter of a two day trek through the jungle.

'It is because it is hard to reach that it is not so popular. Hire a party of the best men you can find, certified guides if you can, but they don't come cheap. You will need at least twelve of them. Then all you need to do Senor is to walk. Then if you are as fortunate as I have been, they will carry many valuable things back for you.'

Charlie, of course knew better. He completely ignored this advice. So after a hazardous flight bobbing fifty feet above the trees most of the way, and a boat trip in a leaking barque hardly capable of staying afloat through dangerous rapids, he arrived at the flea bitten village . Here economising on even spending a night at the only hotel, he hired the first six men that presented themselves for half the money they quoted for the expedition. He promised them an unspecified bonus on his safe return. He thought that this would provide a jolly break from the remorseless book signings and reward him with many wonderful artifacts at a very cheap price.

After only one day of their trip into the jungle his party turned upon him, robbed him of all his possessions. Then forcing him to carry most of the baggage for three terrible days they marched further into the jungle to an obscure part, where they took turns at beating him to death.

Fortunate in encountering the charity of these small brown people he later lay speechless and powerless to do anything for himself in the native hut. The damage had been done, far from having one crack, the golden bowl was now shattered into a thousand tiny pieces that would never again fit together. Charlie was semi paralysed by his awful injuries inflicted upon him by these evil men. He could do nothing for himself. He had to be fed, washed and clothed, and could not even control his natural functions. However, nothing was too much trouble for the indians. From his personal point of view he found this situation to be nothing short of miraculous, wedded as he was to the law of 'quid pro quo', but of course, since the indians spoke no English, the reason for the the excellent care he was receiving never became clear.

Father Gregorio Mancini was the antithesis of everything that Charlie Elliot stood for. Receiving his vocation to the priesthood shortly after taking his first communion, he was one of the youngest priests to graduate from the seminaryof the Augustinian Order in Rome and after training as a doctor, soon opted to devote himself to the salvation of the aboriginal peoples of South America. He had then worked tirelessly in this noble aim for many years, doing much in a quiet way to improve the lot of these primitive people. After running a Medical Mission for twenty years he had asked his superior for permission to pursue a solitary path living and working in the deepest jungles of the continent. On a particular day not long before the beginning of Charlie's fateful journey Father Gregorio had set off from his primitive hut on the edge of the verdant space to make his way to see another similar priest some twenty miles away.

It was a simple accident that could happen to anyone in that sort of place. The good father was well experienced at walking through the jungle and very adept at watching where he put his feet. If a particularly brilliant bird had not been attacked by another iridescent specimen just to his left and fifteen feet away, which distracted his attention he would not have trod upon the recumbent Bothrops Atrox, aka Common Lancehead, aka Fer-de-lance which had been intent on minding its own business. Nobody likes to suffer under the heel of oppression and this, the most venomous species of snake in Central America, was no exception to this rule. It speedily sank its spikey fangs into the good father's left foot. He was dying quite quickly but probably not quickly enough.
  The father had fallen near a shallow stream. In the agony of the snake bite he crawled towards the cooling water and there shortly afterwards expired.

His body was never found, possibly due to the possible presence of Pirhana fish in the gully where the sainted man died. Within a week his absence was noted when he failed to rendezvous with his friend. The monastic order began a systematic search of Father Gregorio's little home and all the places where he was known to visit with no luck. They then began send brothers out into the jungle to contact the small almost extinct colonies of Los Indios in a search that consumed many weeks.

One day, after Charlie had been in the care of the indians for three weeks or more, a man in a white outfit came into the Indian village. The man was Brother Salvatore, a lay brother of the Augustinians order of missionaries. The arrival of such was not a big event in the quiet life of the village, but these men were always welcomed if only for the medical aid and supplies they always brought with them. The brother spoke a little of the native argot and so he was asked to speak to the head man of the little gathering. It was raining, it was nearly always raining so he went into the chief's hut.

'big man we find. him very ill. This man Father Grego, no?' said the elderly small indian.

'you have man now? Him not dead?' answered the learned brother.

'yes, we have man. I show you man.'

153

The little man got up and backed out of the leafy hut.
Understandably Brother Salvatore was very excited and
followed the tiny senior indian to the edge of the small
group of leafy huts in the clearing. In this hut he saw a
man with four weeks growth of white beard, clothed only
in a white gown who was lying on a primitive litter made
of sticks and leaves. Brother Salvatore had never seen
Father Gregorio and had only been transfered into the
mission in the last few weeks having served most of his
time in Columbia. However he was familiar with the
description of the missing man. It must also be
remembered that Charlie's face was much blistered from
insect bites and he had lost much body mass due to his
privations and the spartan fare of the indians.

Within another week Charlie had been helicoptered out of
the jungle and taken back to the main missionary hospital
a few miles down the coast from Cancun where he was
tenderly cared for by nuns of another catholic order. The
extent of his injuries were shocking but no facts emerged
either from the indians or from Charlie, who could not
speak, as to how he had sustained them, but there was one
matter on which there was not a shade of doubt; this was
the true Father Gregorio. A celebratory open air mass was
held in Mexico City presided over by none other than
Cardinal Montez, who was then the most senior catholic
priest on the continent.

Meanwhile efforts were being made to find Charlie. These
were complicated by the furtive manner in the which the
author normally behaved, because before leaving for his

trip he had merely told his tour manager that he would be back in a week, not bothering to indicate where he was going, So the first seraches were rather perfunctory as no one knew where to look. A more diligent approach discovered the pilot of the plane and the river boat captain. The grandee came forward to reveal what they discussed on the fatal evening so an expedition was assembled and equipped but in spite of it spending three months in the wilderness no trace or sign of Charlie was found.

If the brothers had their suspicions about the man found in the jungle they kept them to themselves because Father Gregorio's arrival back in Europe was an enormous coup for the Vatican, beset as it was at the time with all the allegations of kiddy fiddling by the catholic clergy, such a morsel of good publicity had to be seized upon avidly. Had it not been for the inconvenience of him still being alive, canonisation would have proceeded apace. His discovery amongst the indians was considered to be miraculous and already several spontaneous remissions from fatal illnesses had been claimed by members of the faithful who had invoked his name in their prayers of supplication, Even when Charlie's face began to recover from the swelling brought about by the insect bites, the change in his features was put down to physical mortification brought about by his spiritual progress.

The publishers were reluctant to let the fuss die down. As long as there was talk of the missing author and speculation as to his whereabouts the sales of his book continued to be good, so in order to keep the story in the newspapers more efforts were made to discover the secret of his disappearance. Eventually, someone had the brilliant idea of reading the instructions or consulting someone with knowledge of the area and its criminal infrastructure. Ex-commissario Raymondo Lopez was just such a man. Dismissed from the force when his connection with a local gangster became too obvious to overlook and his lifestyle, for so long out of keeping with his pay also became too difficult to ignore, the rather corpulent figure had fallen from grace, not only with the public, but also the police authorities and even the criminals he used to consort with. The good man was sleeping off the previous day's overdose of Tequila on a bug infested mattress in the nastiest hotel in Cancun when his slumbers were disturbed by a knock on the rickety door.

The advance he received was enough to pay off some of his debts, buy him some new clothes and make a start to re-establish a relationship with his estranged family. But for the money he had also to provide a full report of his every movement from day to day and wire vidoes of the places he visited. But $10,000 is not to be sniffed at, particularly when the sum did not include expenses which could be claimed separately. To be fair to ex-commissario Lopez he did make a good fist of the job for he painstakingly followed every stage of Charlie's unfortunate journey to the wilderness. The patient investigator was in no hurry. It took him a week to finally arrive at the clearing on the river where the small settlement lay. In another week and by the expenditure of a hundred dollars worth of Tequila he had got to know most of the more worthless inhabitants of the place, and many who lived in huts further up the river. He was posing as a wealthy local *paisan* who had made his fortune in Mexico City. Soon he was the bosom companion of two of the 'hostesses' in the cantina which was the only social venue in the god forsaken spot.

Subtle enquiries amongst these lovely ladies revealed a rumour that certain men with bad reputations had been throwing money about. Lopez nodded sleepily when he heard this but went on carressing this particular doxie as if the information was only of passing interest. Another week went by and the slow moving Lopez had almost unwillingly listened whilst the girls gave him the names of the six individuals and even their likely abodes. Moving outside the bar he now began to hang around the only shop, which, of course given its locality, sold everything. Here again he assumed his false identity and pretended to be interested in buying the business or setting up another one further up the river. The owner on hearing the astronomical price this '*Idiota*' was prepared to pay, was only too anxious to open up his account books for inspection. Here Lopez was able to find the damning evidence that was required to arrest the six men he suspected, for they had all been freely spending the Yankee Dollar with gay abandon in the past three months. The money had gone mainly on river craft, tackle and new clothes.

The Ex-Commissario returned to Cancun and visited his
former office. What he had to tell the commanding officer
redounded greatly to his credit, given the international
furore concerning the mssing author. So Lopez was
hastily re-instated inot his old rank, put in command of a
task force of ten men, and immediately sent back up river.
By the end of his third week on the case all but one of the
men were in custody, and within another week every
shred of information had been wrung from them. The fate
of Charlie Elliot was at last known. However, in spite of
long and gruelling searches of the part of the jungle where
the men remembered leaving Elliot's body, it was never
found. Raymondo Lopez became an overnight sensation
and serial rights to his story sold for millions which were
then published as a book. A few years later whilst running
for political office he was assassinated.

A conspiracy theory that Charlie had been kidnapped by
the Vatican and held as a perpetual hostage for his anti-
religious views gained currency for a time, but no one
ever suspected how near the truth this silly idea was.

Father Gregorio had suffered a massive stroke. But for the
intervention of the Indians he would have certainly died.
After a year of careful nursing by the Sisters of St Vincent
de Paul it had to be admitted that he was not much better.
With enough rest in between engagements though he
could muster the energy to sit on a comfortable back seat
and be driven in a black Limousine past thousands of the
devout, or even raise his left hand in a feeble wave. It was
enough for a living saint, such as he, only to appear to

make sinners feel better. He never regained his voice although many claimed that when close to his presence they could hear beatific words through the medium of telepathy.

In spite of the heavy burden that the good lord had seen fit to ay upon Gregorio's shoulders he was seen to bear his sufferings with quiet resignation, and that alone was an inspiration to many. His life was held up as a model of charity, obedience and chastity. Pope Benedict said of him

'.. **he represents the spirit of generosity and selflessness which are so out of tune with this secular age where such books as 'Dynamic Pessimism' embody the narrow views of an unchristian majority.'**

Father Gregorio happened to be sitting on the same platform as the Holy Father when he heard these fine words dedicated to him. A young nun tasked to nurse him, who happened to be watching noticed that a slight smile crossed the features of the living saint on hearing those splendid sentiments of the Pope.

The day before yesterday

Being a memoir of a famous local doctor

'He not busy being born, is busy dying'   Dylan

The Carlton Hotel
51 Marine Drive
Eastbourne

Friday July 18th 1987

Dear Frederick.

I hope you are well. Primrose and I are enjoying a pleasant stay at the Carlton Hotel which is situated on the Marine Drive here in Eastbourne facing the sea
I suppose I could have sent you a postcard, but since I enjoy writing letters I thought I would treat myself to a couple of stamps and send you a letter instead.

It being a dry and warmish day we decided to have a look at Beachy Head on Wednesday. This superb promontory is situated well to one side of the long promenade at Eastbourne, in fact from where we were staying a walk of nearly two miles was required just to reach the footpath leading up the cliffs. It was for that reason that we took the car and parked near the little cafe that lies just at the foot of the path.

The walk was well worth the effort. It was most bracing to stand at the edge of Beachy Head and look down. The drop to the sea is over 350 feet at the highest point. Primrose refused to get nearer than a dozen feet from the edge. I felt there to be a tremendous tranquillity at that spot, where so many troubled lives had ended. As you and I, Frederick, are both medical men, the presence and closeness of death is something that we often encounter. Don't you think that we value life far too highly, for what is death but a long restful sleep?

When we arrived back at the hotel, after our stroll, Primrose was feeling a little unwell, so she retired to our bedroom, which by the way, is on the first floor front of the Carlton with a nice sea view. It was such a pity she became indisposed, because we had been having such a pleasant time.

The Carlton is not a large hotel, but it is certainly superior to a guest house. The management run the place to a high standard, all the staff wear uniforms, for instance. Being at a loose end, with Primrose being ill, I decided to have a drink in the bar. The bar is quite small, but pleasantly situated at the front of the hotel. There is seating for about twenty guests in the area, and on that particular afternoon it was very quiet, for apart from myself, there were three ladies sitting in a corner. One of them was elderly and did not look well. She reminded me of one or two of my older patients. The other ladies were much younger. I idly speculated whether this was a mother with her two daughters on holiday together.

Of course there was no draught beer available, so I purchased a bottle of Heineken lager. Don't you find, Frederick, that a cool glass of lager is most refreshing? It was whilst I was sipping this drink that the strange man accosted me

'Do you mind if I join you?' He said. Since my attention was fixed on an excellent book about Toxicology, this sudden intervention (interruption?) rather started me.

However, I did not behold a fearful fiend or even a friendly behemoth, but was confronted instead by an apologetic looking man in his late sixties dressed in a walking coat, pink woolly hat and, somewhat incongruously, with sandals on his bare feet. Stooping, he placed a tray on my table and sat down without being asked. 'You don't generally mind a bit of my company,' he added.

Since the area was almost empty this was a peculiar request, to say the least, but as I did not wish to cause offence, I smiled up at him and said.

'No please, help yourself,'

 My attention returned to my book. Then out of the corner of my eye I saw that he was pushing a glass towards me that contained a pleasant amount of whisky, then another glass with water in it. He took another two such glasses off the tray and placed them in front of himself.

'I always thought it strange that a man that knows so much about whisky as you would prefer Bells. I took the liberty of getting you a double. You can add your own water.'

This was a most unusual occurrence, because professional ethics do tend to keep me out of most licensed premises, and we are warned, even at medical school, to avoid too many interactions with lay people. However the man, after seating himself opposite, was quiet for a few second regarding me with a large smile on his face.

'It's always a bit awkward at first, because you can never remember our other meetings, and I know how you tend to get a trifle alarmed, because I am a bit that way myself, or at least I used to be before my present malady.' He saw my reaction to this statement, and held up both his hands in token surrender, 'No, I am not a hypochondriac looking for a consultation. Your ears will not be beset by a catalogue of medical disasters, of that you can be assured. We have met many times, but in such a way that you can never remember.'

'Do you live in the Manchester area?' I asked. The stranger indicated that he did.

Now it all started to make sense. This man was someone who had seen me many times as we both went about our business, but chancing to be on holiday in Eastbourne, he had decided to use the opportunity to introduce himself. It is often the case that we see a great deal of certain people in local streets or in supermarkets and shops without ever having the chance to speak to them.

'I happened to remember that I would be in Eastbourne on this particular day, but to be honest I never expected to see you in here. So here I am – James Wilson – Jimmy

to some, Jim to many, at your service' We shook hands.
'So how are you today?'

'I'm fine but my wife Primrose is not feeling well.' I went
on to describe our trip up Beachy Head earlier that day.
My companion listened politely, but I could see that he
found my story somewhat pedestrian, which of course it
was.

'What did you think of Beachy Head?' He suddenly asked.

I told him that I thought it was a peculiar place, for one
thing, there were no signs advising against suicide, as one
sees at other spots where the practice of self extinction is
popular.

'Like the Clifton suspension bridge over the gorge of the
River Severn for instance?'

'Yes. The only thing at what I think is the best spot for
suicide at Beachy Head is a sign saying 'Cliff Edge'

It has a bench nearby also, perhaps the seat is placed
there for those with second thoughts or reservations, but
there are no imprecations in favour of continuous
existence. The absence of such suicide discouraging signs
seems unusual in these hyper empathic days, when we
are all supposed to feel so much sympathy for others.'

'If I were to jump off it would make no difference to me,' he said suddenly.

'Apart from the fact that you would be extremely dead,' I remarked.

'No doctor, or rather you are half right. I would only be half dead.'

'Well there would be a body lying at the bottom of the cliff, that some poor public employees would have to pick up and take to the mortuary. It's not a very pleasant thing to behold a body that has been dropped from a great height. For a start the bruising is terrible from a long fall, then all the broken bones gives the body a jelly like consistency, making it difficult to pick up and put on a stretcher.'

'That's the medical man talking,' he said, for he had already guessed the nature of my profession. 'You are a very good doctor, you treated my wife, I remember, and I did see you a couple of times, and will probably see you again.'

It was quite possible that I had treated this man. My current practice was in Hyde, Greater Manchester, but I had practised at Todmorden for some time. I made some none committal remark and looked at the level of whisky in my glass. It was an excellent drink, although I did not wish to rush it, getting away from this annoying chap was becoming an imperative.

' What I am saying is that if I jumped off Beachy Head, I would certainly be dead today, but I would wake up alive again two days before.'

'The day before yesterday?'

'Precisely!'

So that was it, I thought. This whole thing was just an elaborate stratagem by a poor lunatic to get my attention. Switching immediately to consultation mode I eyed him with professional sympathy.

'How long has this been going on?'

'Of course there is no way I can prove to you that my life is going backwards. I could give you many facts about things that will happen to you in the next five years if you like, or I could give you every winner running at Kempston Park on Friday. The problem with these two approaches is that you can only know that I am right by living until that particular day. These facts don't mean anything now, but I will certainly give you those winners then at least in this parallel universe you will make a few pounds from my advice. You see I know everything worth knowing that will happen. I also know about everything that will happen to you doctor.'

Now, this last statement of his took me aback, for we all have our secrets to keep, none of us are beyond reproach. If I do have a fault it may be that I am a trifle to prone to have mercy upon poor sufferers.

I took a different tack by asking him when it started, the strange effect of his perception that his life was going backwards.

'To be honest, I don't remember too well.'

'But you must have some idea or perception of when and how. Was it a Gypsy's curse, for instance? Or to put it another way is there any event in your life that may have triggered it?'

'I do have a theory,' he said in a very sombre manner, 'you see, I was in hospital I think, or at least I'm pretty sure, because it's all very hazy. My first, or if you like, my last memory, was of being very ill in hospital. I cannot sort one day out from another from that time, for they were all the same and I've no idea of how many of them there were. The next thing I recall was being in a home for the elderly, and again it was impossible to tell whether one day was before another or after it. I believe the I was very old at the time. Much older than I am now.'

This very peculiar conceit did bring a smile to my face, I must confess, although I am not known for my sense of humour, as you know Frederick, but here before me I had a man complaining about the fact that he was growing younger!

'You were confused? Perhaps you were suffering from dementia?' I asked.

'Do we have to talk about this?' He said suddenly. 'You always ask me when I first noticed it . . .' He paused. 'You must remember that we have met , and in much less pleasant circumstances than this.'

At this point I began to believe him, I know it sounds like a strange tale, Frederick, but there was something eerily convincing about him. He did not come over as someone suffering from any normal mental malady, he was too articulate, too self possessed, and his interest was partly in me, not being totally obsessed with his own condition. The thing about it was, if I had got the right idea, that his past was my future. The tenor of his remarks being that my life would not be as comfortable for me going forward, as it was at that moment. From then on my questioning became more urgent, in the hope that he might reveal something of what was in store for me.

Looking a little distracted he rose, as if to go. He was impatient with me I could see. I asked him to sit down again. I went to the bar and came back with two more doubles. Bells for me but I bought him a Laphroaig, but I don't know why. Perhaps it was an off chance, the genius of the perverse??

He noticed that one of the glasses had a darker tinge. He picked it up and sniffed the divine aroma. 'You're not supposed to know I like that stuff. What a peculiar thing time is after all?'

'It was a whim, I saw the bottle behind the bar. Can't stand it myself, you might as well add a teaspoon of TCP to your whisky.'

'Do you often prescribe novel cures for everyday conditions?' He asked me. This was another strange question, to which I was at a loss to formulate a reply.

He then said, 'OK, if you really want to know what I think. I'm pretty sure that I must have died in the hospital, and the going backwards started from the moment of my death. Perhaps it happens to everyone? What if we all start travelling backwards from the point of death in billions of parallel universes? Who knows?'

'But you were in the home first, very ill and they sent you to the hospital?'

'Where I duly died at an extreme age, but then the peculiar effect started and the march backwards began. I don't know, I mean, the knowledge of what was happening, must have occurred to me when I finally arrived back in my own home. Now at some point the residential place, for the old and confused, sent me back to the stage before, to my own home I mean. I was still very confused, but not as bad as I had been in the home.

I was seeing a lot of my daughters at that time. I have three of them, good middle aged ladies by then, all taking it in turns to look after the old man. There was only me in the big house. I didn't remember my wife at the time, she was one of your patients – but I told you that didn't I? She died, then there were the home helps that came in. But you see, I had to become aware of the passing of time, start taking an interest in the television, read the newspapers to realise what was going on. I was still confused and I had no idea that every morning when I awoke that I had gone back two days'

'Of course, doctor, you are quite right. Everything starts off from one point and continues. Like the Big Bang for instance, or the way that we all begin as individuals when one specific spermatozoon hits the egg secreted that month by the mother and from there on we are either being born or on our way to the end. From nurses to hearses. Yes my newly awakened consciousness, my enlightenment, if you like, began from one singular occurrence

One day one of the carers didn't turn up. I was not getting around very well at the time so I was left lying in my own excreta for a while. I had been expecting her, but with her not being there . . well I won't go into details. One of my daughters, I think it was Beccie, eventually arrived at tea time and she was not best pleased. She rang the social services to complain. I was listening to her, so I must have started becoming aware by then. Apparently the poor woman, the carer, had been involved in a traffic accident, and been badly knocked about. Hence the 'no show''

'This convinced me that something strange was going on, because, this woman, the carer, well, she was there the next day. But according to Beccie and the Social Services she should have been lying in hospital with all sorts of injuries.

Again, even this peculiar occurrence would not have registered if Euphemia, the large black woman of West Indian descent had not made an impression upon me for she was a very pleasant lady with an excellent sense of humour and always very cheerful. Don't you think, doctor, that cheerfulness is next to godliness? Anyway. you see, the very next day, which was of course, as we know now, two days earlier, the lady came in to see to me as usual.

'Hello Mr Wilson, and how are you feeling today. It's surely lovely weather out there, the sun is shining and god is in his heaven. It will do you real good to sit in the sunshine. I'll takes you out there later, when I gets you all cleaned up, dressed and fed and all.'

'My my! Euphemia,' I said, 'You sure are a tough cookie.'

'What do you mean Mr Wilson,' (that was one thing I liked about Euphemia, she was always very formal, even when giving me a bath or taking me off the toilet.' 'Well!' I said, 'Getting over your accident so quickly. I was told that you were receiving treatment for your injuries at the Tameside Academy of Medical Mishaps?'

An arch look came over her handsome features, 'Why Mr Wilson I thinks you must have been dreamin or p'rhaps you has been sneakin a drop too much of that there Buckfast tonic wine your daughter Beccie brings in for you?'

Of course I know now what had happened, but it seemed incredible at the time, for poor Euphemia had not a clue what I was talking about . .'

'Because her accident had not happened?'

'Precisely, but bear in mind I was no genius at that stage, so I naturally expected her not to come in the next day, because then she would be having the accident, and let me tell you I was a bit surprised when she did come in again. But when she continued to turn up and the accident never happened I got to thinking. I even asked my daughter Beccie about it, but she just looked at me and shook her head.'

173

He sat still for a minute thinking and then took a drink out of his whisky.

'Ah Laphroaig! What a smoky flavour, not had one for years. I shall certainly have another before long,'

'Do you want another?' I said anxious for him to continue.

' I think it was at that point, that I asked my other daughter, Eleanor, to bring in a newspaper for me every time she came. But even then I did not believe it, but put it down to my mental state, because I knew then that I was suffering from Alzheimer's. But slowly and surely, what with the radio and the television and the dates on the newspapers, the truth slowly permeated through into my brain. Of course, the other thing was that as I became younger I got better. A few more days passed by, but remember a week to me is a fortnight in the past, it may even have been longer. And I said to Beccie. "You know Beccie! I think I am getting better, because I don't feel half so confused as I was doing.'

'How did she react?' I asked him.

'She burst into tears and gave me a hug. She couldn't stop crying for ages. I never mentioned it again after that.'

'But you continued to get better?'

'We both know the reason for that. One of the strangest things about human life is that you can get used to anything. Now it seems the most natural thing in the world to wake up two days younger every morning, and there has been ever such a lot of joy.'

I said I thought his predicament must be most frustrating, not being able to finish anything or have any continuity in life.'

'Oh yes I have stopped doing silly things.'

'Did you ever commit suicide to see what would happen?'

'Nothing as silly as that, but I did catch a plane to Prague once, it took ages to get there so I did not have long to look around or drink much beer.'

'You still woke up back at home next morning two days before?'

'But you see, doctor, there are always consequences, as you yourself will find out, or you probably know already?'

'What do you mean?' I asked, thinking to myself, what it was that this man knew about me.

'Each one of us lives in a series of parallel universes. We travel between them constantly. At every turn and twist of our lives we drift betwixt and between them. Most of

them are so similar as to be identical. It is my misfortune
that mine are both extremely particular and time warped
to be that exact day in my previous life. However the thing
to remember is that each one stretches infinitely to the
future. For instance, if I was to have poisoned your
whisky. That first whisky I gave you. The consequences of
this act: you would die, I might give myself up to the
police, do the decent thing, and tomorrow - ?'

'I would be dead and you would wake up the day before
yesterday?'

'But in that particular parallel universe another version of
me would be tried in court for the murder of such an
eminent practitioner and subsequently sent to prison to
be punished for my crime. I would suffer and my family
would also suffer. Primrose, your wife would miss you,
and your patients would also be inconvenienced not to
mention the other ones of course, who would not be
inconvenienced by your subsequent actions . .'

'What other ones - - ' I asked, getting a little hot under the
collar because of all these hints this man kept dropping
about things that he could not possibly know. But then it
occurred to me again, I can be trifle obtuse at times, that
if his ridiculous story was right, and he did come from the
future he probably did know. He stared at me hard for a
few seconds and then smiling he changed the subject.

'But as I was saying there is so much joy. I used to hate family parties and Christmases, but I never miss any of them now, and soon my wife is going to come back to life. How great is that? Also on the last day I see her, before she dies, I will ask her not to go to a certain appointment she has made. She won't die. So in that universe going forward she will still be alive, or at least until she suffers a natural death. Then from then on, we will both be two days younger every day, until we part forever at the youth club in 1965, where we first met.' He looked radiantly happy when he said this.

This last statement of his was most alarming to me, I racked my brain to see if I had ever treated a 'Mrs Wilson' but there were so many.

'You will eventually go back to work?'

'Yes.'

'See your children grow younger and move back home. Meet your parents again.'

'Yes I have all that to look forward to. These days every time I go to a funeral I never fail to look up that person a week or two later. I live in the continuous past you see. My life is always going backwards, but everyone around me is hurtling towards the future.'

'Where you have already been.' He got up from the table.

poor. It was a miracle she had got to the surgery on her
own. I arranged for her to be admitted to Tameside
Infirmary, and went to see her that evening to see how
she was getting on. The cause of death was put down to
heart failure.

And that was about it. I did not bump into Wilson again
whilst we were there, but the rest of the week passed
pleasantly and everything would have gone off splendidly

but for the journey back where the car broke down and we waited two hours at Buckingham motorway services for an AA man , arriving back at Hyde at eleven. Primrose was not best pleased. The AA sent me a voucher for £30 for the inconvenience.

With warmest regards

Harold Shipman

Quigley's Christmas Banquet

Desmond Aloysius Quigley could never be described as a
sentimentalist. He had a good idea when to open his
mouth, but less of when to shut it, but he always reckoned
that the unsaid was far more eloquent than anything put
into words. Which is why he rather despised
Christmas. Not that he did not like to enjoy himself.
He liked a drink and could put himself around a fish
supper with great dispatch. Generous even, providing
someone else was prepared to be dispatched to the bar
and get in the drinks, he would lay out his money all
night. But he preferred to enjoy himself when and
where he liked and rather objected to the sanctioned
publicly endorsed liberties of the Yuletide festivities.
As a frequent habituee of licensed premises he got
rather hot under the collar when people could not
make their mind up about what they wanted to drink.
Solitary in the Stalybridge Buffet bar one festive
period Quigley was standing behind a long haired
individual wearing a Climate Extinction Tee Shirt,
who asked the barman unsure vis a vis ordering a pint
of beer 'Do you think I would like it?'

He was on call that day. Christmas Day 2017 to be
precise. If anything turned up at Manchester Central
Police Station he was to be called in. Alone in his

Alton Currier Lane flat, he was sitting with a tray on his lap upon which was the remains of an Indian Take Out he had not quite managed to eat the previous early morning. To accompany the scant scrapings of Vindaloo Curry and Rice he had toasted two slices of that amorphous white bread that comes in orange packs. He was watching the 9867th re-run of the Wizard of Oz on the telly and had just got to the part where the unlikely party of Tin Man, Lion, Scarecrow and Dorothy were told in stentorian tones to 'Take no notice of that man behind the green curtain,' when the phone rang.

It was a long drive, but at least the roads were quiet on the way to Knutsford. He had to be surprised at the size of the place. A huge Victorian Mansion standing in ten acres of its own grounds. But he was even more surprised by what he saw in the dining room. The huge table containing every Christmas Dish that any jaded palate would relish was surrounded by no less than eight corpses. Some had slumped to the oaken parquet floor, some lay back as if dozing, others lay with arms across the table. It was a most peculiar sight and for a moment it knocked the wind out of his sails. He turned recognising an Indian detective sergeant from Central. 'I suppose, Merry Christmas is the order of the day Tariq, but I have seen jollier ones? Nothing's been touched has it?'

'Only been here ten minutes Mr Quigley, but the fire bobbies were here first. Smell that?'

Quigley had not noticed the acrid odour in the air before. He sniffed and nodded.

'Fire in the kitchen. Deep fryer. Chap at the lodge, you drove past it?'

'Yeah.'

'It's rented out. Anyway he was having a fag outside and he spotted the smoke rising from the back of the big house and called the brigade. Not much of a job, but done a lot of damage. Not that any of this lot will be bothered now.' He waved a dismal hand a the jolly party.

'Was there anyone in the kitchen?'

'Oh yeah! Both dead. Bloke about fifty and a young woman.'

'Talking about being dead. We are sure that this lot have all bought it are we?'

Sergeant Hussein smiled grimly. 'Waiting for the pathologist, but none of them have moved and they all feel cold to the touch.'

'Cause of death?'

'Oh come on Mr Quigley. I am not a miracle worker, but two have been shot the rest are probably poison cases.'

'So you think the food on the table has been poisoned?'

'Why were you feeling a bit peckish?' Quizzed Hussein.

'Not now.' said Quigley.

'That thing on the table is what they call a party bomb. It goes off with a bang scattering coloured tape and confetti and other crap. Just in case you ask.'

'Not too fond of loud bangs myself. Been around guns too much in my time to see much enjoyment in 'em. Hey! It's perishing cold in here. All the windows are wide open, did you notice?'

'Come to think of it yeah, but we might as well leave them open as one or two of these might start going off. What do we do now?' enquired Tariq.

'Nothing,' said Quigley.

The firemen packed up and went home. The local man a police constable patrolled the area at the front of the big house. Quigley and Hussein stood at the edge of the big dining room looking at the peculiar spectacle laid out in there. They had to wait for the Scene of Crime officers to arrive, and even then could not go into the area without wearing the coveralls and masks that would prevent their own DNA from polluting the vicinity of the table.

They stood in silence surveying the grisly scene. To distract his attention from the horrors on the table he began to systematically look around the room. It was large. He estimated the area to be at least twenty five feet by fifteen. The walls were wainscotted in oak up to the high decorated ceiling. On those walls were richly framed paintings which he guessed were originals from the Italy of the 15th and 14th centuries. An elaborate cornice composed of partly gilded white plaster went around the edge of the ceiling where directly above the table from the centre of richly decorated plaster roundel the large chandelier was suspended directly over the centre of the table. At two other points equally spaced there were painted roundels depicting mythological scenes where lots of those delightful male infants equipped with tiny wings displaying their gorgeous infantile buttocks hovered in gay abandon.

'Puttii.' said the Chief Inspector.

'What?'

'Them little chappies with the bare arses. That's what you call em.'

'Oh!' said Detective Sergeant Tariq Hussein hardly bothering to make a show of interest.

'You know what I think. And this is only a flyer, Call it blue sky thinking. I think what we have here is either not enough or too much.'

'I'd say they erred a bit on the excessive, isn't it?'

'Let me finish. Whoever did this, and it is more than likely that one person is behind this. Whoever did this either tried to kill everybody in the world that he or she hated, call that possibility A, or covered up one important murder among all the others. You see what I mean Tariq?'

Hussein looked at the carpet for a bit. His neck was hurting from looking at the ceiling and it was far to grisly a sight to keep looking straight ahead. He hummed and then he hawed before speaking.

'Of course if she, he or it, was a very vindictive person, which from the evidence of our eyes, he, she or it, definitely was, I am sure there were many more people that were candidates for homicide. Whereas, to speak to your other point, if the death of one of the party was required, why murder so many of them?'

But the answer to this largely rhetorical question was left hanging, for at that point what Quigley was pleased to call the 'Circus' had finally arrived. After donning the white suits, foot coverings and face masks the two detectives left the techies and adjourned to the kitchen only to be shooed out of that room also for they had forgotten that there were another two dead bodies in there. They then decided to roam far and wide in the big house.

There were no less than ten bedrooms upstairs, four of which showed signs of habitation. Searches of drawers and cupboards, together with family pictures, did help to identify some of the bodies. As an aide memoir, Quigley drew a diagram in his notebook (see page 4) and entered all he knew about the scene, most of it quite irrelevant. They located a small scullery on the third floor where at last they were able to brew a cup of tea. They located some jam, biscuits and some rather stale bread from which they made toast with jam. By the time they arrived back at the murder scene the senior pathologist had arrived, a man not known to either Quigley or Hussein.

'Come with us. Found a more comfortable gaff,' said Quigley to the tall grey headed chap. 'We will be more cosy and able to talk there.'

The man did not object, particularly when Quigley produced a bottle of whisky that he had 'Found' and added a copious quantity to the tea. Adjoining the scullery was a small lounge, which long ago had probably been used by the servants. 'We would offer you some of the food, cause it will all get thrown away, but in the circumstances, you understand,' said Sergeant Hussein.

'Can't tell you much just yet. Called in another three pathologists. Amount of work there is here, we will be lucky to start moving the bodies before midnight.'

'Yeah,' said Quigley taking a good swig of whiskey and filling up his cup from the bottle.
'But there must be something unusual about this, there generally is?'

The medic, who was taking a cautious sip, removed the cup from his mouth and laughed heartily.

'That's a good one! Tell me inspector when was the
last time, that you attended a case with ten dead

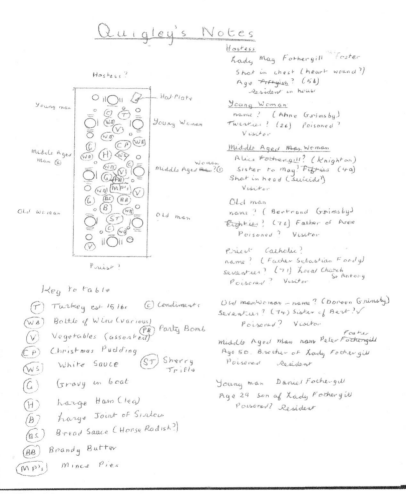

Quigley's Notes

Hostess
Lady May Fothergill ~~Foster~~
Shot in chest (heart wound?)
Age ~~Fiftyish~~? (58)
Resident in house

Young Woman
name ? (Anne Grimsby)
Twenties? (26) Poisoned?
Visitor

Middle Aged ~~May~~ Woman
Alice Fothergill? (Knighton)
Sister to May? ~~Fifties~~ (49)
Shot in head (suicide?)
Visitor

Old man
name ? (Bertrand Grimsby)
~~Eighties~~? (76) Father of Anne
Poisoned? Visitor

Priest? Catholic?
name ? (Father Sebastian Foody)
Seventies? (71) Local Church St Antony
Poisoned? Visitor

Old ~~man~~ Woman – name? (Doreen Grimsby)
Seventies? (74) Sister of Bert? ✓
Poisoned? Visitor

Middle Aged Man name Peter Fothergill ~~Foster~~
Age 50. Brother of Lady Fothergill
Poisoned Resident

Young man Daniel Fothergill
Age 29 Son of Lady Fothergill
Poisoned? Resident

Hostess?
Young man
Young Woman
Hot Plate
Middle Aged man (2)
Woman, Middle Aged ~~Man~~? (2)
Old woman
Old man
Priest?

Key to table
(T) Turkey est 15 lbs   (C) Condiments
(WB) Bottle of Wine (various)
(V) Vegetables (assorted)   (PB) Party Bomb
(CP) Christmas Pudding
(WS) White Sauce   (ST) Sherry Trifle
(G) Gravy in boat
(H) Large Ham (leg)
(B) Large Joint of Sirloin
(BS) Bread Sauce (Horse Radish?)
(BB) Brandy Butter
(MP's) Mince Pies

bodies?'

'No, no, please don't be taking this the wrong way. The inspector he meant no harm by his question but you understand the urgency. If a murder case, she is not solved in two days many moons must elapse before the question is settled.' Tariq hastened to say.

'No offence taken gentlemen I assure you. This is a splendid case. It is like nothing I've ever seen. There was definitely some Cyanide used, Strychnine and there could be others, but the murderer or murderers wanted a quick result which rules out Arsenic. There was a strong odour of Almonds pervading the table. However judging by the facial rictus I would go for Strychnine as it does produce agonising pain at the end. Not a pleasant way to go.'

'Particularly at Christmas.' said Quigley smiled broadly.

'Bah humbug and all that,' echoed the medic. 'Not at any time, but if they suffered they did not suffer long. OK, and do you have any more of that whiskey. I will be here hours yet so I might as well have a drink while the going's good. Right over to you Inspector. What was your name again?'

'Quigley, Des to my chums and I am a very friendly chap most of the time.' The pathologist introduced himself as Christopher Postles. 'Just give me your first

189

impressions and I will tell you if they chime in with mine?'

Quigley showed the pathologist his diagram (see page 4) and the medic put in some of the missing information based on driving licences and personal papers found on the deceased people. 'To sum up, of the eight seated at the table, six were definitely poisoned, as far as we know up to now. The lady in the middle named Alice Knighton was shot in the head and the hostess had a bullet in her chest. Shootings were probable cause of death in both cases. Then we think the two in the kitchen were poisoned, one of the bodies, Mr Dolan reeks of Strychnine.'

'Then there was the matter of the turkey,' said the pathologist.

'It was not on its plate. I should explain that the table was wired with special hot plates to keep the food warm. The turkey stood on a platter and the platter stood on a hot plate near the top of the table near where Peter Foster was sitting. Someone had tipped the turkey and the platter off the hot plate and pushed the face of the hostess Lady Fothergill onto the hot plate. It has made rather a mess of her face.'

'So that rather rules her out as a possible murderer, cause she wouldn't decide to fry her own face would she? Said Tariq.

'Not necessarily, for she might have have murdered one or two off her own bat and then been murdered by someone else.' Objected Quigley. 'Then of course with her face altered it makes identifying her a problem. Perhaps she did the murders absconded and put some other woman in her place destroying the face?'

Fully suited up and masked the two detectives and their pet pathologist returned to the fray which was now buzzing with Scene of Crime wallers. By that time Chief Inspector Gladys Arbuthnot, a somewhat severe lady with the movements of a good welter weight boxer, and Superintendent Siddall had also attended. Both Assistant Chief Constable and Acting Chief Constable were expected to arrive soon. Quigley privately wondered how long it would be before Andy Burnham the current Mayor of Manchester turned up.

'Where were you?' asked Gladys without preamble.

'Hello Sir,' Quigley said to Siddall ignoring the question.

'What do you think Mr Quigley?' asked Siddall, a burly man with a surprisingly gentle manner.

'I think that there are two questions here. Is this a self contained scene? That is, do we have murderers and victims all present?'

'And the second question?' said Reginald Siddall.

'Well it would be difficult to murder all these people so efficiently and then do away with yourself so the second question is: Do we need to look anywhere else?'

Siddall mulled this proposition over for a full minute before speaking again. 'Self contained, you're saying? But what about the catering staff?' Here Gladys came in with a bustling interruption.

'Joe Dolan and his daughter Siobhan, small catering firm, van parked outside. Chap at the gatehouse said they arrived around 11 am, so they must have been in the kitchen a fair while before they put the food on the table in the dining room.'

'Unlucky day for them. Do we have proximate times and causes of death yet.'

'Early days yet, sir,' said Gladys, still hogging the limelight, 'but it is looking like nearly everybody died within a short time of each other. The two in the kitchen look to have been offered a glass of champagne each.'

'Sparkling strychnine.' Quigley commented.

'I had the opportunity to spend a bit of time with Chris Postles, senior pathologist, first on the scene of this motley crew, and between us and Sergeant Hussein we have come up with a scenario. By the way we found a little lounge area upstairs where you might be more comfortable?' The party made their way upstairs to the cosy room. Fortunately the bottle of whisky had been put out of the way. Mr Postles was invited to the mini conference. Quigley despatched Tariq to make the tea and coffee.

Chris Postles was the first to speak. 'I think we can draw a couple of fairly obvious conclusions from the evidence. The gun play happened last. When the two shots were fired six of the diners and the two in the kitchen were already dead or too far gone to do anything. The second conclusion is about what we are supposed to think,'

'Can you clarify that remark?' asked Siddall.

'Yes. We are supposed to think that the middle aged woman, Alice Knighton, sitting mid table to the left of the hostess, organised the poisonings of the others, then shot the hostess Lady Fothergill in the heart and then returned to her own chair and shot herself in the head.'

'The gun was very adjacent, we can do a paraffin test to establish whether she fired it herself,' said Gladys.

'There may have been two guns involved. Anyway I don't think much of that theory.' Quigley remarked.

'As I was saying, ' continued Chris Postles, 'that is what we are supposed to think, and it is a theory that fits all the facts.'

'But it is too neat, If a thing looks to good to be true then it usually is.' said the Chief Superintendent.

'Motives?'

'Money? Hatred – Christmas has been known to bring out the worst in people, but there is one big over riding objection to the theory of what we are supposed to think,' Quigley continued.' and that objection is that it is ludicrous. Why would someone go to all that trouble to do away with the others and then top themselves? For my money we are looking for somebody else here.'

'The eleventh at the party?' said Gladys.

At this point the superintendent took charge. 'OK, this is what we are going to do. We trace all the other members of the family and interview them. We get the lawyers and accountants in, never mind about Christmas, we want to know about inheritance and who stood to gain from the deaths. Then there are the two live-in servants a man and his wife. They were allowed two days off for Christmas. We want them in for a full interview. Regarding the cars parked on the car park at the back we want to know who drove which car and a full Scene of Crime in each car, including DNA. We then want DNA in the dining room and kitchen to exclude the deceased people.'

'Before we go hareing off, there is one peculiar feature that we must think about. Lady Fothergill did not place her face on the hot plate. Someone went to the trouble of moving the turkey, which is a whopper by the way, then they had to get hold of the plate and move that. After which the hotplate was up sticks and move up the table to place the woman's face on it. Why would anybody go to all that trouble?'

With that thought hanging in the air, the little meeting broke up for Reginald Siddall was anxious to brief both Assistant Chief Constable and the Chief himself who were both present on the premises. This was an extremely high profile crime and was certain to make both national and international news.

But the Chief Constable had gone by the time Siddall got back down to the ground floor. The Chief Constable had come, he had seen, and if he had not conquered he had at least consulted. The Chief Superintendent was told that the Assistant Chief Constable wanted to see him in the car park. Richard Burton, for that was his name, was sitting on the back seat of a large black car. The engine was running and his police driver was ready to move off. Siddall was given the impression that the time of the said Richard Burton, Assistant Chief Constable of Greater Manchester was very valuable indeed. Siddall was made to stand and address the high panjandrum through the open window of the distinguished vehicle.

'Perfectly straightforward case this Siddall. That woman, the one sitting in the middle?'

'Knighton?'

'Yes that's right. She poisoned the rest of them, shot the hostess and then shot herself in the head. I think you will find her finger prints on the gun and the calibre of the bullets recovered will match. Get some background on her and you will find that there is a family feud or something, she is the aggrieved party, revenge killing and all that. You should have everything wrapped up by lunchtime tomorrow. Brief me at 1230 say and we will have a press conference at 1400. Make us look good this will. Remember the world is watching Manchester. Is there anything else?'

'No sir.'

'All right driver!' with that the stately vehicle pulled out of the car park and the ACC was gone.

Leave was cancelled the next day so back at the Manchester Central Police station Mr Quigley and his two acolytes, Detective Constables Judy Wilson and Joe Jones were sitting at their usual table in the third floor canteen on the morning of a rather fine and sunny Boxing Day. Judy Wilson was a tall willowy blonde who tended to stoop because she was self conscious. Working with Quigley had made her more confident. Joe Jones, fiftyish, a misfit like Quigley worshipped his boss who had rescued him from being the station's dogsbody.

'We generally go for a family walk every year in Heaton Park on Boxing Day, then we have a little party with Sherry Trifle at Grandma's place.' commented Wilson bleakly.

'I was booked in to see the panto at the Opera House with Edna's lawyer friends. It is an office tradition. Second year for me, then they go for a meal somewhere. The partnership pays.' Added Jones with equal bitterness. Edna Shorrocks was Joe Jones's girl friend who worked as a Clerk for a prestigious firm of Manchester Barristers.

'So you are both far better off here with me,' concluded Des Quigley. 'Now let me build you up to speed -' at which point he gave his two excellent colleagues a run down on the main aspects of the grisly scenes at Knutsford. 'Right Jonesey you are on the door steps. Mr Siddall is holding a conference so you will be delegated to a team to interview relatives of the deceased and so on. Cut along, for according to my Mickey Mouse watch the meeting starts in five minutes.' Jones got up from the table masticating his bacon sandwich as he made his way to the door. Quigley continued, 'Now you and I, my little chickadee, have been deputed by no less an authority than 'Close the door Richard' Aka Richard Burton, Assistant Chief Constable to investigate the affairs of the late Alice Knighton, so look alive and follow me!'

A very run down 'bijou' or 'studio' flat in the
Levenshulme area of the city, was their first port of
call, where the dead woman had spent her last years,
There were only two rooms. A tiny bathroom with
microscopic sink, toilet and stand up shower. The
other room, not that much bigger, combined: Kitchen,
Diner, Bedroom and Lounge. Although clean, the
place had that musty smell of genteel poverty and
unexpressed grief. Rifling through her possessions
they came up with a few papers and photographs of
happier times then it was time to journey back into the
centre to see the lawyer.

Messrs Ponsonby and Ponsonby hardly boasted a
distinguished office, overlooking as it did the old
Apollo Cinema across Ardwick Green. They climbed
the creaking stairs to be shown into a small office
containing one desk, at which sat a man who could
have auditioned for the part of Scrooge in any
production of 'A Christmas Carol'. All around were
piles of files all resting on the dusty wooden floor and
all looking likely to collapse at any given second. For
a start he was wearing a wing collar, a style not seen
since the nineteen twenties. A black suit shiny in most
places. His hair was silver and worn long but in need
of washing. He had a pronounced stoop and on his
nose was balanced a pair of pinc nez.

'Welcome to our humble offices. How can we be of
service?'

'You deal with the affairs of the Fothergill Estate?'
said Quigley, at the same time looking at the appalling
state of this untidy room. 'And you are Mr
Ponsonby?'

'Weathers my name. Albert. The Ponsonbys, were of
another age. Yes we endeavour to handle the affairs of
estate. Quite a lot of money tied up you know. By the
way what a terrible business! Were you there
yesterday?' here he raised his eyebrows. 'I can see
that you were expecting a more palatial setting, but
these things cost money, I find that Miss Grant and I,
you saw Miss Grant downstairs? Miss Grant and I
manage tolerably well in these premises.' Mr Albert
Weathers was eventually persuaded to tell Constable
Wilson and Chief Inspector Quigley the history of
Alice Knighton.

'Well connected family the Fosters, two girls and a
boy. Money came from the Cotton Trade. May, who
became Lady Fothergill, and Alice two years her
junior. Peter never did much but leached on the
family. They were all privately educated of course. He
at Eton and the girls went to Roedean. Alice was
affianced to a soldier, Colonel of the Guards. They
were to marry but he was killed at Goose Green,

Falklands and all that. Although they never married she took his name Knighton. Alice was left expecting a child, big row in the family. Strict moral code big church people. She had the child adopted, but it made no difference. They wanted nothing more to do with her. Alice drifted into bad company, drugs, did a bit of smuggling for a boyfriend, Maltese he was – silly girl ended up in Holloway doing five years. Then when her parents died she was cut out of the will. May and her brother Peter got all the money. On the other hand her sister May married into money, Frozen Food -Cod in Butter Sauce and Peas. Her fortune goes into the tens of millions, husband dead.'

With this masterly summary noted down they took leave of the frowsty office and made their way back to Central where they were immediately ushered into the presence of Reginald Siddall who was sitting in his office with his head in his hands. Gladys Arbuthnot was sitting looking very pensive. Siddall raised his head and indicated that the two should sit down.

'You might as well go first, Quigley. What did you find out about Alice Knighton?'

'Well! She had a motive I suppose. But she might easily have gone there to forgive and forget. Anyway big trouble in the Foster family, didn't like her boyfriend, she preggers etc. Hostess is her sister, Lady

Fothergill. She got all the Foster money on top of the fortune from her late husband. Alice has form, living in squalor etc etc. Hard luck case. Depends how you look at it but she could be said to have a motive, but how she went about doing it is an entirely other matter.'

'Good work Desmond. Completely wasted, but I am sure that the ACC will be pleased to hear that his pet theory was validated.' here he paused before bestowing a meaningful glance on Gladys.

'Shall you tell them Miss Arbuthnot or shall I?'

'A body has gone missing,' said Gladys.

'What?' said Quigley and Constable Judy Wilson almost simultaneously.

'I haven't told the ACC yet.' said Reginald Siddall looking down at his desk.

'Perhaps they've lost it. I mean there was a lot of dead bodies. I would imagine that they would have had to rent space somewhere to store them?'

'They knew late on last night,' put in Gladys, 'but they wanted to be certain. They have searched every hospital mortuary in Greater Manchester, and every ambulance and found no trace of the body.'

'Do they know which one it was?' asked Judy Wilson.

'They are pretty sure it was the caterer's daughter Siobhan Dolan that has gone missing.' Chief Superintendent Siddall was not pleased with life that morning.

'Why should someone want to pinch a dead body?' asked Gladys Arbuthnot.

'Ah that is assuming the body was dead. It all changes if we assume that body was alive, then what is to stop it walking away by itself?'

'That same thought did occur to us, Desmond. And it further occurs to us that it blows the ACC's precious pet theory, with which you and Constable Wilson have been wasting your time this morning, clean out of the water. Right this is what I want done, immediately or before. Check the identities of all the dead bodies to make 100% sure that they are who we thought they are. Then I want all the toxicology reports done as soon as possible. I will leave that to you and Miss Wilson Quigley let me have your report, signed sealed and delivered by four this afternoon is that understood?'

Quigley and Gladys liaised in her office downstairs briefly. 'Reginald is going mad. This case has advanced his retirement by a year or two. Go and see Sergeant Hussein at Knutsford. They have set up an incident room at the hall. He has a finger in all the relevant pies.'

'I hope all the meat is Halal then,'

Instead of going direct to Knutsford Quigley and Wilson decided to check out some of the addresses of the deceased first. Photos of the cleaned up corpses had been forwarded to Wilson's computer so it was fairly easy to ask anyone living close to a given address if this or that was a good likeness to the particular deceased. The first place they visited was the premises in Tarporley, from where the late Joe Dolan had conducted his catering business. The place consisted of a shop, closed on Boxing Day, but there was a phone number for orders prominently displayed on the window. The recorded message stated that the firm was currently closed for the holiday. They were no further forward in tracing the home address.

Across the busy trunk road was a small general shop and off licence run by an Asian gentleman.
'Yes' he knew the Dolans, father and daughter. Yes he knew where they lived but was vague about the

address. It was somewhere in Wythenshawe. Bardsley Avenue or was it Beardsley?

A full hour later they ran it down by dint of knocking on nearby doors. As it turned out they were the first police people to arrive and break the bad news. Mrs Dolan was distraught with grief. She explained that she had seen the news on the television and had been trying to contact the police ever since. They were asked to sit down and share a cup of tea. The small council house lounge was gaily decorated and in the corner stood a Christmas Tree with lots of unopened gift parcels underneath it.

'We always keep Christmas of Boxing Day. There is only the three of us, Siobhan, Joe and me.' she explained. The sight of the gifts nearly brought a tear to Quigley's eyes but Wilson was unashamedly weeping. (There is something about Christmas, even if one hates it, that gets to you every time.) Things took an interesting and even more poignant turn when the lady, Mrs Dolan said that picture of the dead girl lying the kitchen was not her daughter. For a few moments the poor woman had grounds to hope that Siobhan had survived. She was brought back to earth when showed a picture of the body of the young woman at the table who was thought to be Anne Grimsby.

'Yes, that's my Siobhan,' she sobbed.

They waited a while comforting the widow, she gave them Turkey and Stuffing Sandwiches saying that there was nobody else there to eat anything she had prepared. Quigley noticed that Judy Wilson, though a vegetarian did not have the heart to refuse the food. Eventually a police woman specializing in Grief Counselling arrived to help to console the poor bereaved lady. Quigley and Wilson said goodbye.

Back in the car on their way to Knutsford Quigley spoke. 'So this is how it was done. There is this somewhat nefarious young lady, call her Miss X. She decides for whatever reason to murder all the party at the Hall including the catering staff. We don't know quite yet how she did it. But lets say she waves her magic wand and they all drop off the twig together – stone dead. She then goes into the kitchen with a bottle of bubbly and offers Joe and his poor daughter a drink laced with Strychnine. She then goes back into the dining room and shoots the hostess Lady Fothergill in the heart, and Alice Knighton in the head with the revolver. She then presses same into Alice's hand to make it look like she fired the gun. As an extra bit of malice, or to confuse us, she presses her Ladyship's face onto the hot plate. Finally she changes clothes with Joe's daughter Siobhan and places her body at the table in the place reserved for Anne Grimsby. She then, dressed in the kitchen gear

lies down on the floor and awaits developments
pretending to be dead. Later loaded up in the
ambulance she makes her escape. Bee bo bended my
tales ended.'

'So we only need to find Anne Grimsby and we have
our murderer?' said Wilson.

But after their arrival at the hall, Sergeant Tariq
Hussein soon stuck a pin in their bubble, when he told
them that a certain Miss Anne Grimsby had been
found murdered in her luxury flat in Didsbury.
Hussein was puzzled. 'She can't have been murdered
twice surely?' Quigley appraised Hussein regarding
their discoveries, and the sergeant saw the light. '

So your Miss X sets off by murdering Miss Grimsby
then goes to the hall here in Knutsford with some
trumped up tale of Anne's illness and being sent in her
place, which they obviously swallowed and invited
her to stay for the meal, then the rest of it was done
more of less like you said.'

The case dragged on for two weeks accumulating a
mountain of evidence, but not getting any closer to
tracing the mysterious Miss X. There was a
photograph of her lying on the kitchen floor dressed
up as Siobhan Dolan, but it was taken at a funny angle
and was not much use in identifying her. It was

published in all the newspapers and shown on TV to
no avail. A year later the whole matter was quietly
dropped and filed with all the other unsolved cases
that bedevil the crime statistics Only Quigley was to
discover the truth and then from the very unlikely
source of his closest friend, a career criminal by the
name of Frank Warren who controlled the whole of
Greater Manchester's illegal drug network.

There was no way the pair could risk being seen
together in public, so every three months or so
Quigley would wait in some convenient place, within
staggering distance of his abode until he was picked
up in Frank's stretch limousine always driven by
Frank's most trusted man, little Alfie. Then in the
Mink lined interior, during a pleasant hundred miles
drive, they would get pleasantly plastered together
from the copious on board bar in the vehicle, while
talking of old times past in the East End.

After a while Frank broached the subject of the
K***sford Killings (as he styled them). 'You'll be
pleased to know Des that I has got to the bottom of
that partikiler can of worms. One of my mates down
the smoke told me over a few pints, no names no pack
drill, about this girly who worked at Porton Down,
you know that place where they tests out all them
nasty nerve gases and so on. Anyway this geezer, call
him Bill if you like, says the girly wants a good dose

of this stuff placing in this party bomb thing, so when it goes off it fills the room with the deadly stuff. Bill generally makes proper bombs. Don't use them much myself but a bomb can be a very handy thing if you uses it right. Anyway my mate Bill thinks it a highly unusual request, but two thousand nicker is hard to come by, without working for it, so he thought what the hell? Anyway the girlie impresses him as a real hard nosed little bitch. Then this nerve gas was top of the range, and a highly secret secret. One breath and you are a gonner. It had another peculiar property of leaving no trace behind. Fooled the pathologists completely'

'I'd made a study of this case cause you'd given me most of the grisly details and it occurred to me how could all those people get dead so quickly. As if they all died within a few seconds. Poisons don't work that way do they?'

Quigley whose nose was buried in a very large crystal glass full of Glenmorangie Twelve year old Special Reserve, decided not to interrupt Frank, who had got into his full narrative flow.

'You told me about all the winders being wide open when you arrived, and that party bomb thing being on the table, so it all clicked in my mind. She must have either held her breath or worn something. After the explosion, she goes into the kitchen, poisons Joe and his daughter, gets in the dumb waiter, so as to get well out the way for a bit, to let the gas clear. She comes down and opens all the windows before substituting the body of Siobhan and doing all the other stuff, like spraying some Cyanide and Strychnine around and putting her Ladyship's face in the old frying pan.'

'Perhaps she takes some stuff to slow her breathing down, before lying down in the kitchen, make her look more dead? Can't have been much fun when they stuck that spike into her liver to measure her temperature, but still!'

'Good stuff this, but can I water it down a bit?' Quigley referred to the whisky and Frank handed him a tin of Carlsberg Special Brew.

'So as I said it got me interested in running her down and finding out why she did it. My mate Bill had a photo of her, which he took on the sly, then I had to check the records at Porton Down but I finds her. Cost me a few bob I'll tell you, but a man has to have a hobby. Turns out she was Alice Knighton's illegitimate daughter. Name of Joan Baker, after her foster parents. She has it in for her mother, getting her adopted, for she has this unbelievably bad childhood with a kiddy fiddling foster dad. He turned up dead, by the way, but that is another story.'

'Young Joan studies, goes to college, chemistry, job at Porton Down. Meets boy, marries, two children. On holiday in the Lake District when there's a car crash. Husband and children killed, other car drives off unscathed. Joannie had a headache, so stopped at their digs so wasn't in the car. Driver of other car turns out to be Lady Fothergill, but one of her servants a certain Joe Dolan says he was driving the car that day with his daughter. Then some friends of Lady F who were staying at the same hotel as her.'

'Don't tell me, let me guess, the Grimsbys and the priest, Father Sebastian Foody.'

'Yeah, that's right they all swore blind that Lady May Fothergill was with them all that afternoon on a trip to Lake Coniston. So what with Joe Dolan coming clean about borrowing the car with his daughter and the Grimsbys, their testimony clears her ladyship, but Dolan serves three years in prison. The rest of the family all help to hush it up. When he gets out a certain sum of money changes hands'

At last Quigley speaks. 'So she plotted the perfect revenge to kill them all to make up for her childhood suffering and the loss of her family. Do you know anything else about her Frank?'

'Can tell you where to find her if you like. No skin of my nose.'

'And why on earth would I want to do that?' said Quigley.

*** *** *** *** ***

Leaving Home.

Me and Batman go back a long way. My ninth birthday treat was a trip to the cinema to see the Batman film with Michael Keaton as the man himself and 'Jack' as the immortal Joker. In the foyer, after the show, Ma bought me this Batman bobble head doll. It was not much of a thing but it meant something to me. Looking back it symbolised a time when my parents expectations of me were not astronomical and I was allowed to be just a kid. When I ran away from home the doll was one of the things that went with me. But before we get to that bit, a bit of background info will come in useful

Batman was a misfit and so was I. The debonair and slightly vacuous dilettante Bruce Wayne was a million miles away from the brooding presence of hooded

213

avenger. Is this making sense so far? Perhaps not. They say writing about yourself is the most difficult thing. According to a writer buddy of mine, someone who makes a good buck out of writing, it is easier to pull out your own teeth than write your biography. Anyway that is one excuse, and it will serve until a better one comes along.

Everybody blames their parents for fucking them up. Why should yours truly be the exception? Me and my buddy, the writer, you remember? We always had this big argument. He said that everybody is basically the same, driven by the same emotions, urges and whatnots and heading in the same direction. But for me everybody is different with different emotions, urges and so on. We never could agree on this point, but sensed that we were both right (and wrong) at the same time. Which brings me right back to Batman and how our epic journey began..

Ma and Pa were as different from me as it is possible to be. Roseanne my sister, who was two years my senior, was stamped from the same sheet as the elders. The deal was that the three of them were super brains, whereas with me, the brain cell supply was strictly rationed. Dad was an oncologist, mum a paediatrician, and, at the time of the parting of the waves, big sister was in first year Med school. It was assumed that I would follow in the family profession and take my place in the ranks of the physicians and surgeons, but things had not gone so well in my studies. That year saw me in the 11th grade in High School, but my parents had wanted me to take the SATs (Standard Assessment Tests) a year early. These SATs

215

are tests to get you into college, which in my case would have been pre-med school. Most kids take their SATs in the 12th grade, but my parents were ambitious. My brilliant sister had taken hers in the 10th grade and as a result was the youngest student in her year at Med School.

I had struggled all the way from kindergarten. They had hired expensive tutors and spent hours of their own time keeping me up to the mark, but the mark just kept on getting further out of reach and there came a point when no matter how hard I tried the power was just not in me to pass any more tests.

A day or two before things came to a head, Ma was on the phone to the mother of a class mate.

'Leo has Heppleman's Syndrome it is a rare B complex deficiency disease which even in quite brilliant students can affect academic prowess.'

This was news to me. I was raiding the fridge when I heard this conversation, having been grounded for a fortnight and banned from playing on my computer or watching TV for failing the SATs so miserably. Nobody was speaking to me. When I entered a room they all wrinkled noses like I had crapped in my pants. As I said Ma was a paediatrician, which is some kind of children's doctor, so when she talked about childhood diseases, folk listened, but just the same? Heppleman's Syndrome??? Still from her point of view it was better to lie, and make up a mythical disease than admit to having a distinctly average son.

So another couple of days passes when everybody is trying to make out that Leo is not there, or when he is, that an elephant has just crapped on the carpet, and I am invited to a meeting with my father. Now Pa in those days practised as an oncologist, these are doctors who deal with the disease of Cancer. Old pa must have been an expert at giving people bad news. Such as:-

'Well Mr Schultz there is some bad news and some good news. The bad news is that your tumour has doubled in size, but the good news is that we can sign you up to four weeks of radiation therapy that will make all your hair fall out and make you feel like shit, followed by twelve weeks of chemo that will make you

feel even worse. But cheer up! Because we rate your chances of a full recovery at over 25%'

The news that he delivered to me was not good. 'Now son I won't say that we, your mother and I, are not disappointed, for that would not be true. You have had every chance, the best tuition that money can buy. We have supported you through every stage of your education and in spite of all our efforts you have just scraped through your SATs, but your marks are so poor that none of your choices of Universities can be honoured. But now at this vital stage, with your career in the balance - '

 I think you can fill in the rest of the speech for yourself. The drift was that I was a runner up to the average person with learning difficulties and not far short of only being fit to live in an institution. But they still had plans for me.

Pa told me that I was being sent to a crammer, where I would spend the next twelve months revising to pass the SATs, at the end of the 12th grade, and if, even at the that stage my scores would still not get me into pre-med, there was always the options of Dentistry or Pharmacy. Now how did I feel about that?'

I had been looking at the carpet, whilst he spoke. Living at home in the last few years had made me behave like a trustee in a prison. The efforts of Ma, Pa and Big Sister, not to mention all the caring professionals that had tried to 'help' me over the years, had worn down my Self Esteem and natural dignity. The 'Trustee Rules' were simple:

Never make eye contact with the screws, touch your cap to everyone and look after those rose beds just outside 'D' wing like your life depended on them, pick up all the dog ends left by the visitors, and keep out of the way of the rest of the prisoners, as far as possible.

'Sounds like a plan,' was muttered before I left the room, determined not to give him the satisfaction of seeing me upset. The thought of a year spent doing millions of IQ tests, Calculus, Algebra and learning to spell gazillions of words with nothing to read but Shakespeare, Melville, and Thomas Wolfe, was a prospect that made suicide look attractive.

We were living in Anaheim at the time. I was a student at the High School, where I was classified as a 'Nerd' in spite of my unpretentious academic aspirations. I only had two friends, one a fat African American called Dwayzee, and the other a small Jewish kid called Isaac.'

You know how black kids are all supposed to be super coordinated and athletic? Well poor old Dwayzee had a job with his shoe laces, and the only things he was good at catching were colds. Little Isaac also did not fit the racial prototype either, because unlike most Jewish kids portrayed in the media, he was neither bright nor glib. We were all misfits, the three of us, but we had something that all the sports jocks and the high achievers did not possess. We were aware of the wonder of life, and the opportunities that would one day come our way. We shared the mystical belief that existence was a miracle and every sensation that came the way of our senses was unique and had to be savoured to the full extent of our

limited sensibilities.

To avoid the other kids, whom we found crass and boring,

we used to meet in the library and 'converse' by means of

notes. Nobody bothered us there. The 'Jocks' despised the

library, whilst the Whiz kids were too busy working on

their double A grades to worry about three dead legs like

us wasting space in the old book palace. We drank tea

solemnly in a small seedy place on the edge of town and

talked about everything except the three banned subjects

of : College Football, Baseball, and anything to do with

our education. That left an amazing amount of stuff we

could talk about, but our main subject was how to avoid

conforming to the way we were supposed to behave. We

were all great readers and adopted obscure authors like

Neville Shute, Michael Arlen, and John Galsworthy. We were also very big on Salinger's stuff, admiring Holden Caulfield as a god, and even trying to talk like him,(and all). But our true hero was Yossarian from the novel Catch 22, because we all wanted to grow up to be just like him. The deal with Yossarian was that he knew the truth and was trapped in a bad system where everyone but he was blind or deaf to reality. In that we thought we resembled him.

This tight knit little club of ours broke up three weeks before my flight from the nest. Dwayzee's Dad, who was a big manager at Disneyland, got a transfer on promotion to the Florida branch of Disneyland, one week, and my other chum Isaac was killed in a senseless auto mobile accident the very next week. A rusting old Mustang driven, fatefully by a drunken sports jock, the QB of the high school team no less, mounted the pavement and neatly sandwiched Isaac against an old oak tree. He was dead before the medics got there.

With their passing, one of the principal reasons for my staying in Anaheim was gone. Ma and Pa were amused at my wanting to attend the funeral of Isaac and could not understand my 'adolescent' grief, neither could they understand why the departure of Dwayzee filled me with such sorrow. For so-called sensitive medical professionals they displayed the finer feelings of a Sherman Tank. As for my sister, she had long given up the effort of trying to fathom my deviant nature.

The old rucksack used for my trips to school would serve. First thing in the bottom was the Batman model, then the Swiss Army (imitation) pen knife that Dwayzee had bought for me the previous Chrimbo. The small phylactery that Isaac had fashioned to contain a scroll which bore the opening words of 'Catch 22' . I opened the tiny leather pouch and read the words again, **'It was love at first sight**.' Replacing the scroll I kissed it, just like a Jewish person would, and placed it reverently in the bag. A change of underwear, one jumper, a water bottle, which did not get filled because big sister was in the bathroom. Life savings of $15 and 25 cents in an old leather purse, lastly a pair of socks, I could not think of anything else, anyway the road was calling, and there was not a second to waste.

Ma's voice floated down the corridor from the kitchen,

where she was supervising the preparation of dinner by

Juanita our sulky Mexican maid. 'Where are you going

Leo, dinner is nearly ready?'

'Got to go out for something, won't be long,' I called, then

legged it up Las Palma Avenue in the direction of the road

going North that joined the Riverside Free way. Putting

out my thumb I was lucky to get a lift after ten minutes.

An old Derby and Joan in the auto, he driving, she paying

attention in the passenger seat. Telling them that the bus

back to Artesia had left without me asked them if they

were going West?

'Why son,' says the old guy, 'Fraid we will not be much use to you. Heading North across Riverside towards La Habra.'

'Suit me fine,' I lied, 'My mother's brother lives there, Uncle Eli. He will give me a lift home tomorrow.' The driver turned to his wife as if to ask her what to do.

'He seems a nice clean boy, Elmer, I reckon we should give him a lift.'

'Well!' Elmer drawled, sounding a bit like James Stewart, 'there's a condition son.'

'What's that,' was my reply climbing into the back seat.

'Just make sure you ring your Ma, just as soon as you get to your Uncle's place.'

'Sure thing' I said and we set off. The couple were talking about the death of Dorothy Lamour that had taken place a couple of weeks before.

'That only leaves Bob, cause Bing died back in 1977. Say weren't those road films just great?''

They were surprised when I joined in about Dorothy because real old films used to be favourite watching for Dwayzee, Isaac and me. 'They would have made an eighth but Mr Crosby died like you say.'

We continued to discuss this great trio as the car trundled along at speeds varying between 20 and 25 mph until. La Habra was reached, beautiful down town La Habra to be exact. I was anxious to get out and continue my flight to freedom, but the old couple were having none of that, they regarded me as a child-in-arms and likely to be swept away by any quirk of fate, or even if the wind blew a bit too hard, but having been to the town precisely twice and having the confidence that infects all juniors of the species, my main motive was to get away.

'Your uncle will be picking you up?' the old girl said.

'No, he kinda expects me to make my own way there.'

'Surely not,' says the old guy.

We wrangled over this for a few minutes but eventually I agreed to phone and ask him to come and pick me up. Getting back to the car I said, 'Uncle Abraham's car is broke down, but don't worry he is going to send a taxi.' By the way I had ordered a taxi just to get rid of this pesky pair.

The old lady narrowed her eyes. 'I thought you said your uncle was called Eli?'

'Oh sorry, Eli and Abraham are brothers, they live together and since they work at the same place they share a car.' The conversation would have been prolonged even then, but out of the corner of my eye a taxi was seen approaching. 'Bye folks, thanks for the lift,' I sang and ran towards the cab.

The cab driver turned out to be another unmitigated pest, but this time in a nasty, not a well meaning way. Telling me that his minimum fare was $10 dollars, he kicked me out of the cab after a miserable five miles or so which he spent complaining about his wife. I asked him to head for the Holiday Inn near Fullerton where I knew I could pick up Interstate Five. La Habra (the avocado capital of the world) would have to wait. So after walking another couple of miles I arrived at Fullerton.

Anybody will tell you that pedestrians are banned on Interstate roads so I had to discover a road near Interstate

5 which fed traffic onto the big road, then find anybody that was prepared to take me South. I had chosen the Interstate because that is the road that goes due South along the whole coast of California. It was a breeze. Altogether it took me two months to get to La Jolla which is near San Diego, which is about as far South as anyone can go and stay out of Mexico. And before you ask, No! I did not walk or hop all the way. Things got kinda complicated and it was easier to go with the flow than kick against the pricks (how about those for a couple of mixed metaphors?)

Coming back to that first night I soon ran out of ideas. Nobody wanted to stop and pick me up and the hour got late. The later and the darker the less chance anyone would take a chance, There was a big hamburger joint, guess it must have been a MacDonald. It was surrounded

by low scrubby bushes to make it look more rural, Getting

hungry by then, for according to my watch, my great

adventure was entering its third hour, and I must have

travelled at least fifteen miles from the old homestead. So

I crawled into the bushes and lay down. After a while I

took off my jacket and bunched it to go behind my head

like they do in the cowboy films. By about half of twelve

things quieted down some and eventually sleep came, a

restful night considering the circumstances but with an

abrupt awakening around the hour of seven next morning.

That must have been the first night I ever spent in the

open, my folks were not big on the outdoors so I had

never been camping, Some red ants had got into my

underpants. Panicking I ran into the Big Mac place, right

234

through into the John. Not waiting to get into a stall I shed

my clothes there and then as soon as the door shut. The

Hispanic cleaner (male) thought it was the most amusing

thing he had ever seen. A little blonde teenage kid dancing

around naked in big rest room like some sort of gay

dervish showing all his goods off for all the world to see. I

wish I could have shared his humour.

'Ees OK. Non El fuego hormiga. No bitey'

He was a little tubby guy. He stopped swamping the floor

and followed me around picking up my clothes. 'Agitar

los apagado.' He demonstrated, shaking my clothes, as the

ants fell out of my pants and scattered on the tiled floor of

the large restaurant bathroom.

'Gee thanks.' I said struggling back into my gear.

'Ees OK!' he said again with a smile. He watched me as I washed, even to the extent of providing me with a clean bit of soap from the cleaning trolley. After that walking through the restaurant I tried to look casual. Just as though having red ants in my pants was an everyday occurrence. Weighing up the chances as accurately as possible I noticed that the burger place stood near a slip road that led directly to the interstate route. I walked down the road apiece and began to stick my thumb out at approaching auto mobiles but soon discovered that there was a bend on the road at this point and that it was not a good place for a car to stop. Retreating back to a spot nearer the restaurant I took my stand again with beckoning thumb.

236

After a half hour or so nobody had stopped, offered to pick me up or even slowed down. Rapidly becoming convinced that invisibility cloaked me, discouragement set in. Suddenly feeling a crushing fatigue I sank to the ground and sat on the grass near the road verge close to tears. All the events of the last two weeks, the loss of Isaac, Dwayzee's departure and the dreaded SATS, the way my parents had behaved, all crowded together in my mind. It was the September of my seventeenth summer. Why did life have to be such a bitch? What was so wrong with me that fate had singled me out for persecution? Staring at the patch of road closest to my feet I must have sat in that position for an hour or so, oblivious, and no longer caring whether anyone picked me up or not.

Something nudged my shoulder. Looking up suddenly I
recognised the guy from the bathroom, the cleaner. He
was standing next to me on the roadside, he had
something in his hand. It was a Big Mac with a side order
of fries. Dumbly I took the package from him. It had not
occurred to me to be hungry until that point. He sat down
next to me and watched as I ate. I mumbled some thanks
and offered him some of the change in my pockets. 'Ees
OK!' he said again for the third time and quietly continued
to watch me eat. After a while he spoke again. 'Ees gratis,
Carni et tortilla, ees gratis, no pay' I smiled and gave him
a thumbs up sign. 'a done vas?' he asked me.

'San Diego. I reckon to go to San Diego.' I told him. He
nodded and smiled brightly as if he thought this was an

excellent choice of destination. After a while more of watching me eat he spoke again.

'Necesitas letero' he said. Then he repeated it louder and slower. 'NECESITAS LETERO!' Spanish was not one of my strengths, although I had been taught some at Grade School. Seeing the look of non comprehension on my face he mimed a rectangle in the air and then made rapid squiggles in the imaginary space . Comprehension dawned rapidly.

'A sign?' I asked. Miming my own large cardboard cover for a placard.'

'Si' said the little fat guy, 'Ven con migo!' he got up. Having finished my brunch I got up and followed him.

The thing about the places with the 'Mac' jobs (such as MacDonald eateries) is that nobody ever notices anything. To interact with the rest of world you need to feel that you belong there, have a stake in the place, but when you are working for minimum dollar, plus all the fast food crap you can put away on a ten hour shift, your attention drifts. The world goes out of focus. Sure, you read the corporate stuff in the free papers, about how the guys that run outfits like, Hooters, Wendy's and Walmart are going around improving the lives of the wretches that have to work there, but they never convinced me. A punch on the nose would have sold the idea or even a 'What the hell do you think you are doing in here?' But the blank passive response of the staff in the joints, combined with the indifference of the guys supposed to be in charge, only

240

confirmed my theory. I often speculate how they would

have reacted if I had gone in there with two five gallons

drums of gasoline and started spraying it around before

burning the place down?

So me and my new friend drifted through the place, then

behind the counter into the big store room fridge with all

the stuff still packed up in big cardboard boxes. There

must have been fifty million hamburgers together with the

lumps of pallid frozen fish, deadly white chicken. Cheese

slices (Sleaze chices – in that case) not to mention all the

little anaemic buns they serve the stuff in, the pickles,

salad and gallons of tomato sauce. All these goods are

stacked up in there in the foggy freezing huge fridge. My

friend just rips off the side of one of the boxes to make a

big sign for me. Then he waltzes over to a small desk and

rips off a couple of fibre pens before leading me into the

restaurant area where we commandeered a table.

My placard when ready looked like this.

'Go Aztecs.

******

Young place kicker

needs lift to San Diego

to join football program

****

Go Aztecs

A gang of sports jocks had infested the place a few minutes before, getting off a coach that was heading North towards Orange County. They represented some obscure high school football program and were all dressed in the requisite strip of smart blazer and grey slacks. The coach proclaimed the party as Gately High 'Cougars' Football Team. Football is a great equalizer and many kids from well underprivileged backgrounds can use it as a ladder to hoick themselves up the social scale a few places, I would never knock it, but, I guess, nature never intended me to be a sportsman.

'Say'? I began, edging my way onto the end of a bench seat occupied by a couple of guys who were tucking into a pair of jaw expanding hamburgers that must have been six inches deep.

'Yeah' one of them sprayed at me.

'I'm a big football player and I am on my way to San Diego to join the team there.'

A kid of about sixteen, was seated next to me, whom I took from the size of him, to be a defensive player, blonde with a bad skin, probably obtained from eating the sort of chomping gear he was currently consuming. This guy looked at me and said.

'The Aztecs? That's what the San Diego players call themselves, just like we are the 'Cougars' You must be pretty good if you are joining a college program?'

'I don't like to boast,' said I wondering if I should suit the attitude by polishing my nails.

His mate, much scrawnier but taller now joined in the conversation.'

'Guy must be a kicker, Fred. Stands to sense, he's not big enough to be any use for anything else.'

'Longest kick was 60 yards, but that was in Denver. Altitude, thin air, very!' I remarked. My two new friends were impressed.

'I don't understand kickers,' said the scrawny one. 'If I had to kick to save a game with two seconds on the clock and I missed. Well I guess I'd just sort of die.'

'I never miss.' I said, somehow keeping my face straight.

They both laughed. The big one gave me a friendly shove which nearly had me on the floor. 'You are so full of shit.' I liked these two, for high school sports jocks they were a couple of princes. Most of the ones back at Anaheim High did not speak to people like me, but there again I was pretending to be one of them. We chatted along quite happily until it was time for them to get back on the coach. 'Let us know how you get on, Fred and Jerry at Gately High, will always find us.'

'Sure thing,' I said with fingers suitably crossed. After that I put myself around another monster helping of junk food provided by my Mexican friend, (well I sort of assumed he was Mexican because he did speak Spanish.)

Borrowing some more fibre tips and getting to work in earnest it did not take me long to produce this terrific poster. With a 'vaya con dios' I left the burger place and shook hands with the little fat guy, who had been such a big help.

Believe it or not it takes me just five minutes to get a lift, might have been less. Sort of just wandering down to the bit of road before the curve which was only a quarter mile from the Interstate I had hardly had time to get a stiff arm from holding up my sign before this big SUV is pulling up and a guy wearing a New York Yankees cap and dark glasses asks me to get in.

'That's great,' says I, carefully stowing my poster on the back seat. Looking around nervously I saw that there is only this guy and me in the vehicle. He is maybe fifty and has a bit of a gut, but nothing gross. He is wearing a Hawaiian type shirt that is very wide and covered in many colours, it looks incongruous next to the Yankee cap. He drives down the slip road and soon we are bowling along at a steady 55 mph going due South. Not sure whether I should say anything or not I remain silent, ten minutes later he has not said anything so I opened up the conversation.

'Are you going far?'

'Depends,' he said mysteriously.

'Well I just sort of wondered where you were going to drop me off. I mean nobody expects to be taken all the way, like?'

'To be honest . . ' he began after a couple of minutes, 'There are one or two things I need to see about on my way South, but if you are not in any too much of a hurry?'

Let me tell you, this put me into a bit of a fix. How did I know that this guy was not some sort of pervert. Why, I might end up suspended from a meat hook in his cellar while he chopped bits of me off with a chain saw?

'Well . . ' I began uncertainly. My imagination running ahead of me. 'Perhaps it's better if I just get out and somebody going direct will take me a few miles.'

'Look kid! Let me just drive on for a couple of miles. There's a great place where they do steak and French fries in about twenty miles. I will treat you to a meal and explain the deal. If you don't like it you can easily get another lift from there, cause everybody loves a football player.'

'OK, but you don't have to be buying me a meal a coffee would be just as good.'

'Let's see!' he said and we drove on in silence.

So we stops at this place just off the free way that is done up like a big log cabin. Considering it had about fifty tables no log cabin was ever built that big. Frankly the whole log cabin scene is pretty phoney. Have you ever tried to pick up a tree, for instance. The log cabins they have in the movies are only sets and if you ever did have to build one, a crane would be needed to lift the huge tree trunks into place. We go in, and soon a large woman dressed in buckskins is hovering over our table. 'Two coffees sweetheart and two steak specials.' the guy says to her.

'Is that with eggs over easy and well done steaks?' she queried. He confirmed and cast a glance at me.

'Does that mean if you want a rare steak you have to have sunny side up?' I asked.

The man and the waitress shared a bemused glance. 'Works for me,' he said and gave her a broad wink. In the years since this happened the logic still escapes me.

The meal when it came was pretty good. Steak cooked in chicken fat with two fried eggs and a host of French fries. I made a fuss about paying for it and got out a couple of five dollar bills but he waved them away.

'Bill Grindley,' he said and offered me his hand. I told him my name and we shook. 'The deal is .' he said after he had cleared most of the food on his plate whilst I was only working around the edges of mine. 'The deal is that my head honcho has let me down, and I have a couple of jobs booked in for the next two or three days but I am heading to San Diego. Now if you could see your way to labouring for me it would be a good deal for us both. You end up with some pocket money and I get these jobs done and get paid. Capice?' I considered this for few seconds and we shook hands. His grip was dry and firm. That somehow re-assured me.

After continuing down the free way for 50 miles he turned off it. A few more miles along a good road when he turned onto a dirt track that seemed to lead nowhere, but through deep treed narrow ways that climbed and descended with indecent frequency. I made no comment for Bill obviously knew where he was going, but my fears of being kidnapped, or even done away with, increased dramatically. But there was something re-assuring about him that told me everything was going to be OK.

253

All this time I had no inkling as to what his trade might

be. Any tools he had I guessed must be in the boot of the

large vehicle. Most tradesmen in my limited experience

had big vans or trucks to accommodate all their tools and

stuff.

'Say how far is this place? Bit out of the way isn't it?'

'Out in the wilds. These fringe type of people tend to like

to have plenty of space.'

And that was the start of it and then my life began.

Books by Jim Watson available on
Amazon Kindle. Titles, formats, links to
Amazon Sites, prices and short summary
plots.

The True History of the Dearborn Chainsaw Massacres –
paperback
https://www.amazon.co.uk/dp/B0B6XHXQTB
Cost £5.50
American Meat – What a treat. (ebook version of above)
https://www.amazon.co.uk/dp/B081QX4ZRQ Cost £0.99

Let me put this as clearly as I can: this book is great!
It is by turns tragic and darkly hilarious. The story
starts off with Marvin, a man in search of uncovering

the truth behind the Texas Chainsaw Massacre. The deeper he gets drawn into his obsession, the more the real story unfolds as we are transported back to the time the events in question occurred. We come in contact with various people, all of whom are well developed throughout--the writer does a masterful job of giving life to his cast of characters. As the action progresses, we are helplessly drawn into its gravitational force. You'll find yourself unable to put the story down as you follow the story's arc from rural Pennsylvania to Texas and maybe--just maybe--all the way to Woodstock! But you'll have to read to book to see what ultimately happens. I don't often write reviews; indeed, this is my very first. But I had to write this one because the story was such a wonderful and wild ride! This is a "Must Read!"

Quigley in Trouble – ebook
https://www.amazon.co.uk/dp/B0B71PLZFN Cost £0.77
Quigley in Trouble – paperback
https://www.amazon.co.uk/dp/B0B71ZFRKP Cost £10
(Sequel to Quigley goes North)

Sporadic raids by armed gangs on shopping centres and supermarts are leaving many dead. Quigley rescues his friend Frank from the clutches of such a gang and gets himself into trouble again with the police authorities. Suspended from duty he returns to London to find the person behind these constant plots to discredit him.. Meanwhile back in Manchester a dead body turns up in a canal. His team back in Manchester get to work on this mystery. Can there be a connection between the two cases?

Quigley goes to the North – paperback
https://www.amazon.co.uk/dp/B0B6LLM8LR Cost £9.03
Quigley goes North (same as above) – ebook
https://www.amazon.co.uk/dp/B083ST69GG   Cost £0.99

Disgraced and demoted, dedicated sleaze merchant Des Quigley is sent North to a corrupt police station in Manchester. Teaming up with discontented Kenny Devlin they set about causing chaos. Soon they are up to their necks in murders and mayhem.

Eastman's Retreat – ebook
https://www.amazon.co.uk/dp/B08K3BPS7K Cost £0.78
Eastman's Retreat – paperback
https://www.amazon.co.uk/dp/B08JZWNHCT Cost £17.08

This is the story of the young man who became Richard Eastman. Through force of circumstance he has to leave his home, then his job and finally his country as a fugitive in the British Army. Sent to France as part of the British Expeditionary Force he eventually joins the retreat to Dunkirk and what is known as Operation Dynamo. But this is not a story about the war. It is about family, love and loss. It is about bigotry and cowardice. It is about kindness, friendship and betrayal. It is about deceit, brutality and fear. Finally, it is about courage and hope. Sometimes the fortunes of war form the backdrop and sometimes they are front and centre. But this is the story of one young man's battle to survive in peace and war. This is a sweeping tale full of character which takes the reader along at pace, wanting to know what happens to Richard Eastman and those he meets along the way. I must declare a connection to this book because I know the author and worked with him over 20 years ago when he first began to develop this story. After reading a draft of the first couple of chapters I encouraged him to proceed with it and have done so on and off ever since. I didn't write any of it and have no financial interest in it. I bought my own copy and this is the first time I have read it in its entirety. I believe, therefore, that I am entitled to write a review. All my reviews are impartial; the author in this case would expect nothing else. This book has been a long time in the making but the end result makes the wait all the more worthwhile.

Joe Santini – King of the Woods – ebook
https://www.amazon.co.uk/dp/B08SKC5LGK Cost £0.77
Joe Santini – King of the Woods – paperback
https://www.amazon.co.uk/dp/B08SGR2XKW
Cost £11.01

This is the story of a young west- coast American runaway and his acquaintance with a colourful and resourceful retirement- home resident who has a Mafia history. The story features an interesting updated version of the King of the Woods myth found in the Sir James Frazer's book "The Golden Bough". In most Mafia fiction it is the men who control their women. In this book it is Joe Santini who after a misadventure with the Mafia finds refuge in the exclusive attentions of the Sisters of St Antonia. Realising gradually that they have the whip-hand, he desperately seeks to escape. Perhaps a case of too much of a good thing?